nothing but a set of eyes for stars

NEW WRITING SCOTLAND 41

Edited by
Kirstin Innes
and
Marjorie Lotfi

Gaelic editor:
Niall O'Gallagher

Association for Scottish Literature

Association for Scottish Literature
Scottish Literature, 7 University Gardens
University of Glasgow, Glasgow G12 8QH
www.asls.org.uk

ASL is a registered charity no. SC006535

First published 2023

British Library Cataloguing in Publication Data

A CIP record for this book is available
from the British Library

ISBN 978-1-906841-54-6

The Association for Scottish Literature
acknowledges the support of Creative Scotland
towards the publication of this book

Typeset in Minion Pro, Sofia Pro, and
Noto Sans Canadian Aboriginal by ASL
Printed by Ashford Colour Press, Gosport

CONTENTS

INTRODUCTION

It's simply stunning that this is the third of my New Writing Scotland issues, and the end of my time as co-editor. These three years have passed slowly – at times at a snail's pace – and they've also passed in a flash. The writing we've considered in that time has also come full circle. For the past two issues, we received a lot of pandemic writing, reflecting on the state of the world (and our own micro-environments). While it was important that we acknowledged that unique time in issues 39 and 40, we also felt a real reticence to include too many of those 'pandemic' voices, knowing that we, like our readers, also needed an escape from that reality and reminder of more 'normal' times, whatever that meant.

The work submitted for issue 41, however, felt different to earlier submissions: braver, more edgy, less aggressively embodying of the safety we all sought during the pandemic. Instead, so much of the writing submitted (and selected) peeks through the cracks of doors, pushes boundaries, asks the reader to step out of the known and comfortable. As always, it was incredibly difficult to choose just over forty pieces of writing from the hundreds and hundreds submitted and we had a difficult time whittling it down to the very fine pieces included here.

Like the world around us, the poetry selected for this issue looks again at what we thought we knew well, things that are familiar but also somehow changed. Nasim Rebecca Asl's memories of Persian food lead her to reflect on the passage of time in a family context, for example; Lynn Valentine's 'A Car Draws Up' takes the reader to a familiar place but also identifies what is missing (those who held our hands 'are nowhere near'); and Ryan Van Winkle's 'Flight Path Away' reminds us that no matter how confident we are about finding our way back home, 'there will be a final leg, a one-way trip towards a time when / no map will help [us] plot a way'. John Duffy's 'Average contents, 48' looks again at something familiar, in this case our hands, while Jay Whittaker's poems remind us that re-entering this familiar and equally unfamiliar world can be as out of place as an abandoned ice cream van in midwinter – how 'One shove . . . / plunged me headlong / down this steep, wooded bank. / I lie in pieces . . . / I long for spring.' Jay's other poem, 'Mistaken', also flags the frail and often indiscernible line between life and death, speculating that things we assume long dead are instead hibernating, simply 'shrivelled in . . . spirals to survive.'

The fiction in this year's section also manifests a certain post-pandemic sensibility. Time and again as we read through the submissions, we met characters on the edge – of change, of social tightropes, of their nerves. Time and again, our skin prickled – reading these stories is not a cosy experience, this year. Almost every story crackles with tension, or anxiety, and often that is rooted in latent body horror, whether the awareness of a growing tumour in Claire Deans's 'An Unkindness of Ravens', or the filthy fingernails of the father in Julie Rea's 'Cannibals' – even the joyous, sensual awakening of Amy Stewart's 'The Orange' is overwhelmingly, swooningly corporeal. Perhaps we have become more conscious of our physical selves, their limitations, just like the protagonist of Katie Webster's 'Skin Taste Touching,' all too aware she's trapped in a body in a psychiatric ward.

Death, illness, claustrophobia and decay stalk these stories, from Lucy Cunningham's heartwrenching 'Swedish Fish' to the slow-dread reveal of B. A. Didcock's creeping, unsettling 'The Birthday Parties'. And these are haunted pages. There are many, many ghosts. Covid is almost always there, even when it isn't mentioned; surely the all-too-realistic horrors of a community plagued by rats in Julie Laing's terrifyingly plausible 'A Mischief' (which will crawl up your skin and stay there, be warned) could only have been dreamed up after the unsettling times we've been through.

Yes, unsettling times seems about right, and it's a delight – albeit at times a terrifying one – to see how Scotland's writers are chronicling them.

NEW WRITING SCOTLAND 42:
SUBMISSION INSTRUCTIONS

The forty-second volume of *New Writing Scotland* will be published in summer 2024. Submissions are invited from writers resident in Scotland or Scots by birth, upbringing or inclination. All forms of writing are welcome: autobiography and memoirs; creative responses to events and experiences; drama; graphic artwork (monochrome only, of suitable size); poetry; political and cultural commentary and satire; short fiction; travel writing or any other creative prose may be submitted, but not full-length plays or novels, though self-contained extracts are acceptable. The work must not be previously published or accepted for publication elsewhere, and may be in any of the languages of Scotland.

Submissions should be uploaded, for free, via Submittable:

nws.submittable.com/submit

Prose pieces should be double-spaced and carry an approximate word-count. Please do not put your name on your submission; instead, please provide your name and contact details, including email and postal addresses, on a covering letter. If you are sending more than one piece, please group everything into one document. **Please send no more than four poems, or one prose work.**

Authors retain all rights to their work(s) and are free to submit and/or publish the same work(s) elsewhere after they appear in *New Writing Scotland*. Successful contributors will be paid at a rate of £25 per published page.

Please be aware that we have limited space in each edition, and therefore shorter pieces are more suitable – although longer items of exceptional quality may still be included. Our maximum suggested word-count is 3,500 words, and the submission deadline is **Monday 31 October 2023.**

Gail Anderson
A SEASON FOR WHEAT

The last tenants told me, so I felt obliged to say.

Dan wasn't a believer. Yet here he was: dawn, bolt upright, blankets flung. A sweat-pouring, heart-pounding panic. Stevie asleep in the next room, and Dan half out of bed, ready to carry the boy out the window, onto the porch roof to safety.

Safety from what, exactly? Outside, the wheat murmured, their old white farmhouse in the centre of it. Peaceful, just as he'd hoped.

He closed his eyes and made an effort, steadied his breathing.

The house has a history.

Last week when the old landlord told him, Dan wanted to laugh. He was grateful that Stevie was out of earshot. Down at the bottom of the yard, head bobbing, grubbing around with a stick. He wouldn't have heard. The boy had been through enough.

'I appreciate that,' Dan said. 'Thank you.'

The man's eyes were floured with cataract. Palsy jingled the keys as he dropped them into Dan's upturned palm.

Nothing harmful, mind. The last folks stayed fourteen years.

They'd chosen their rooms. Looked at the views from each of their upstairs windows. Grain, stretching to the horizon. A distant silo. A small, rusted windmill. Country, but just twenty minutes from town. A rented house, temporary, and the boy had seemed less listless already. The country air, perhaps. Change of scene. Take his mind off his mother.

Looks just like the real thing.

Dan's bedsheets were clammy, his t-shirt clinging. Crisp morning air reached him through the sash window, like cooling breath on a fever. Sunrise, an uppercut of orange on the ceiling.

How had it come to this? This lonely house, with its severance smell of fresh paint. They'd all been happy, six weeks ago. Dan's eyes stung. He turned away from the window and looked back into the dim room.

A boy stood in the doorway. Dark hair, short-cut. He wore jeans, a green t-shirt, scuffed leather shoes. A country lad, husky, not lanky like Stevie. His face glistened with sweat, like he'd run all the way from town. One hand on the back of his neck, his lips moving fast, his mouth forming words. All this Dan could see, but there was no sound, no sound at all beyond the whispering wheat. Dan looked away, rubbed his eyes. Took reassurance from the dawn. When he looked back, the talking boy was gone.

Happened some fifty years back.

Sitting on the edge of his son's bed, Dan saw Stevie smiling slightly in his sleep. It was the only time he smiled, these days. In sleep.

Last night though, when Dan had tucked him in, he'd seen a spark.

'If this is his house, where does he live?' Stevie's voice was bright.

'The old man? In town, near the post office.'

'No.' His eyes shone. 'Is there another farmhouse somewhere? He must have come through the field.'

'Who?'

'Showed me where the frogs are, right there at the bottom of the yard.'

My wife never really got over it. We never do get over a thing like that, I suppose.

Stevie was at the kitchen table working through his third bowl of corn flakes, wolfing it down. He seemed to have grown.

'What's your hurry, son?'

'Going to the woods.'

He tipped the last of the milk from the bowl into his mouth. Dan poured coffee from the pot. Looked out the window at the fields. Wondered what the little windmill was for. He'd assumed its blades were seized; today they were turning, just.

'Woods?' Dan asked.

'Bottom of the next field, there's a little valley. Can't see it from here.' Stevie rose, rinsed his plate, placed it in the drainer. His mother would have been pleased.

He looked up at Dan. 'Want to come?'

The boy needed a haircut. Could use some new shoes, too. Dan flushed. Had he actually *seen* Stevie since it happened?

He squeezed his son's shoulder.

'Good idea. I'd like that.'

The last folks were happy here. I hope you will be too.

Stevie led the way, down an almost invisible footpath bordering the next field. Dan walked behind. His boy's arms were outstretched like aeroplane wings, his fingers brushing the wheat tops. This expanse of grain, ripening, drooping. It would be felled in the coming weeks. Combines lumbering up and back, hawks hovering on thermals, hunting exposed mice. And what then? The soil turned under. Snow. Spring ploughing. New seed, a new season.

They made their way down the shoulder of land, each step revealing another inch of green on the horizon. Ash, birch, a small congregation of trees in a hollow. On the slope beyond, the comb of an orchard, orderly rows. Stevie ran ahead, shouting into cool shade, and Dan followed, felt the cushion of loam underfoot, smelled earth and summersweet. She had loved summersweet.

He would take Stevie into town later. Groceries. New clothes. A bucket of white paint. The back porch could use a touch-up and they could do this themselves, no need to trouble the old man. Maybe they'd think about getting a dog.

Dan wasn't a believer, no; but beyond the trees, the pulse of the day beat a little harder. He would let it in. He would let the boy open his eyes.

Nasim Rebecca Asl
ACROSS FROM ME, MY MAM

Laughter at the smell of joojeh kabob, spices
she now calls familiar, home in this strange city.
Her hand wraps around the wine stem

like my infant fingers once held hers.
We toast the mezze's arrival and she tells me, again,
of how she found my name: for nine days she pecked

at Persian books, bland sandwiches, slops of soup
splashing on hospital trays. She salted foreign sounds
over the incubator, her Mackem tongue stumbling

with each new letter and her newborn baby's brittle breaths.
Machinery hummed, her mint gown danced, when, finally,
she whispered her chosen name over my sleeping head.

Now, a breadstick dipped in Shiraz, she tells me
why I suit the syllables: *You are a breath
of fresh air. My summer breeze.* Now, still silent

I smile back. Sip. Don't ask if she regrets her choice.
All the storms that have seeped from me
have been mopped from our Persian carpets by her hand.

I have been a hormonal hurricane, a lost tsunami
racing, raging, door to door. I spewed tornados that ripped
through the fragile quiet of her home. Now, three decades later,

fissures have gathered in the porcelain of her face.
She wears it well, this evidence of her ageing. With each
new season she kneels by the bath, bows her head

over acrylic and stains herself with henna. Coaxes life
back into her hair. Last week, I texted her a photo of the first
silver strand I plucked from mine. I don't have any dye

but she told me not to worry. Now, in this restaurant
the shadows of my empty arms stretch across the table
as she offers me her last kabob.

joojeh kabob: chicken kebab

NINI KHOMKHOMU

a fable among the people of Urmia

When I lived, their hisses slithered behind me.
Torshideh. Jendeh. My pickled hips an empty
promise. Soured. I loved, and loved,
bedded and bedded, peeled open
my heart, my legs, again, again

trying to find my way to that other promised world.
To you, sweet bache, koochaloo. I was born to be maman.
I died with empty arms, degh kard, withered breasts,
all my unbroken waters still churning at my wellspring.

I cling to mountains as my unborn babies
should have clung to me. Earth shakes
when I sob. In the valley where my barren body
rotted, families grow to fear me.

In death their whispers call me Nini Khomkhomu.
Nightjars call warnings from Judas trees
when I wake with dusk. They cry like cicadas,
watchful as serpents, their stony feathers glaring.

Branches drizzle me with petals – soorati for my dokhtar –
and blanket my path. My bare brown feet bloody.
I croon lullabies to the moon. Tulips bow as I pass.
Starstorms crown me silver. I glow white and bright
like sorrow among the trees when I hear it:

mewing, wailing, screaming. Answering the summons,
I blaze back to life, arrive at the side of a cradle
staring at a miracle. Its sleeping parents cannot hear her;

my new daughter weeps only for me. In my arms she settles,
fat fists in my hair. I drop a tear on her forehead.

My nini, baba, peri will never grow old. She clasps
my hand as we roam every forest, her siblings,
all rescued, all taken, all cherished, flocking around us,
squabbling like pigeons, trilling with larks and nightingales,
babbling with possibility. We dust ourselves in sumac,
the sun turmeric on our skin, we count eagles, owls,
the heavy-set bustards roaming our uplands,
we chant ka ka ka with the cuckoos as month after month
we find crib after crib. We rescue the babies
no one else will care for and I carry them all –
their futures, their talents, their promise –
balanced like love, heavying my hips.

torshideh:	like torshi, a pickled vegetable garnish, meaning soured, used to describe unmarried women who are nearing the end of child-bearing years; similar to spinster
jendeh:	slut, whore
bache:	child
koochaloo:	cute one, little one
maman:	mother
degh kard:	to die from heartbreak, verb
soorati:	pink
dokhtar:	daughter
nini:	baby
peri:	in Persian mythology, a fairylike being, similar to a fallen angel

8

Shelagh Campbell
AN TEAGHLACH

"Eil an duine agaibh a-staigh?' dh'fhaighnich am balach.

Choimhead Raonaid air a cùlaibh.

'Tha,' dh'fhreagair i, 'ach chan urrainn dha bruidhinn riut an-dràsta.'

Bha coltas mì-chofhurtail air a' bhalach air an stairsnich, is e ann an deise a bha co-dhiù dà mheud ro mhòr dha. Bha e air chrith cuideachd – nearbhasach, shaoil Raonaid, no fuar 's dòcha. Feumaidh nach robh e fasanta san latha an-diugh stocainnean a chur ort fo bhrògan mar siud, a bha cho biorach, gleansach.

Dè an aois a tha e, smaoinich Raonaid, a' dèanamh coimeas eadar am balach agus Chris, a mac. Bhiodh Chris na b' àirde, ach nach robh esan a-riamh na b' àirde na balaich eile sa chlas aige?

Ochd bliadhna deug, shaoil Raonaid, no fichead aig a' char as aosta. Sa chiad obair aige, is e fhathast a' fuireach còmhla ri mhàthair – cò eile a chuireadh filleadh cho ceart, cho dìreach na bhriogais?

Fhad 's a bha am balach a' feuchainn ri uinneagan ùra a reic dhi, rinn Raonaid sgrùdadh air pìos pàipeir a bha a' stobadh a-mach às a' bhaga ùr, leathar aige. Dè bha an tiotal ag ràdh?

Reic, Reic, Reic!

Liosta de na dòighean-reic as fheàrr, an e? Liosta de na dòighean as èifeachdaiche airgead a ghoid bho dhaoine aineolach?

Ghabh Raonaid ceum a dh'ionnsaigh a' bhalaich. Thòisich esan a' bruidhinn na bu luaithe, is cuideigin a' gabhail ùidh anns na h-uinneagan aige mu dheireadh thall.

Cha chuala Raonaid facal mu dheidhinn uinneagan ge-tà, is i fhathast a' feuchainn ri pàipearan a' bhalaich a leughadh. Dè bha siud air a' chiad loidhne? Phriob i turas no dhà.

Na . . . no an e ma a bh' ann? Sin e.

Ma dh'innseas iad dhut gu bheil na h-uinneagan a th' aca an-dràsta math gu leòr, can riutha . . .

Can riutha dè?

Mhothaich Raonaid nach robh am balach fhathast a' bruidhinn. Bha e a' coimhead oirre, is a' feitheamh air freagairt bhuaipe. Ged a bha Ailean, Chris, Eilidh agus Olivia bheag a' feitheamh oirre air beulaibh *Bargain Hunt*, bha a sròn a' cur dragh oirre.

'Tha na h-uinneagan a th' againn an-dràsta math gu leòr,' thuirt i.

Rinn am balach fiamh-ghàire, is coltas air gun deach cuideam mòr, trom a thogail bho ghuailnean.

'Uill,' thòisich e . . . ach stad e a bhruidhinn gu h-obann. Choimhead e seachad air Raonaid, a-steach dhan trannsa dhorcha.

Chlisg Raonaid cuideachd.

'An cuala tu siud?' dh'fhaighnich e, is mì-chinnt na ghuth. Cha do thachair seo air an latha-trèanaidh aige.

Bha beul Raonaid tioram. An robh cuideigin san taigh? Agus ma bha, dè seòrsa taic a gheibheadh i bho bhalach cho òg, lom? Bha i mothachail gun robh am balach a' coimhead oirre, ach bha ise glacte ann an trom-laighe leatha fhèin.

''S dòcha gun do leig an duine agad às truinnsear no rudeigin?' thuirt am balach, nuair a dh'fhàs e soilleir nach robh Raonaid a' dol a bhruidhinn no a ghluasad.

'An duine agam?' thuirt Raonaid mu dheireadh thall, is coltas oirre gun deach a dùsgadh bho neul. 'Seadh, seadh.'

Thionndaidh i a ceann gu slaodach, ach cha tàinig fuaim sam bith eile bhon taigh.

'Seadh,' thuirt Raonaid a-rithist agus chrath i a ceann turas no dhà, mar gun robh uisge na cluasan.

'Uill, tha còir agam tilleadh dhan teaghlach agam – chan eil mi airson do chumail, is na h-uinneagan agam math gu leòr.'

Choimhead am balach sìos air na nòtaichean a bha a' stobadh a-mach às a' bhaga. Ged a bha e a-mach à sealladh, bha fios aige gun robh seantans aig bonn a' chiad duilleige, ann an litreachan mòra, tiugha. Bha Steaphan, am manaidsear aige, air iarraidh air

an luchd-reic uile an seantans siud a chumail air mheomhair:
Dèan cinnteach gum faigh thu cothrom dol a-steach dhan taigh
– cha deach uinneagan a reic air an stairsnich a-riamh.

Bha e eòlach gu leòr air an sgriobt, is iad air leughadh troimhe
iomadh turas air an latha-trèanaidh. Nam faigheadh e a-steach
dhan taigh, bhiodh cothrom aige dealbhan is sampallan a shealltainn
dhan bhoireannach seo. An dèidh dha prìs ro àrd a thairgsinn dhi,
chuireadh e fòn gu Steaphan agus leigeadh e air gun robh e a'
sireadh lasachadh-prìse dhi.

Bha rudeigin neònach mun bhoireannach seo ge-tà – rudeigin
na sùilean.

Leig e osna bheag às. Bhiodh e na b' fhasa dèiligeadh ris an duine
aice, shaoil e.

'Tha fios agam gu bheil an duine agaibh trang,' thuirt e, 'ach saoil
am b' urrainn dhomh sampall no dhà a shealltainn dha . . . dhan
dithis agaibh? Tha sinn a' tairgsinn barganan sònraichte an-diugh
a-mhàin – chan fhaigh sibh prìs cho ìosal a-màireach no an ath
sheachdain.'

Bha e coltach gun robh e doirbh do Raonaid anail a tharraing.
Thug i sùil air na h-uinneagan aig beulaibh an taighe gu luath, ach
bha na cùirtearan fhathast dùinte. Lean sùilean a' bhalaich sùilean
Raonaid agus ghabh esan ceum air ais.

'Ò, tha mi duilich,' thuirt e ann an guth cugallach, is aodann cho
dearg ri na ròsan a bha a' fàs fon uinneig. 'A bheil . . . a bheil an
duine agad na chadal, no . . . *tinn?*'

Bha Raonaid an impis rudeigin a ràdh nuair a chuala an dithis
aca brag eile bhon taigh.

Chuir Raonaid a làmh ri beul, mar a bha i air taibhse fhaicinn.
Dh'fhàs a sùilean cho mòr ri truinnsearan.

Ghabh am balach ceum eile air ais. Ge b' e dè chanadh Steaphan
ris, cha robh e deònach dol a-steach dhan taigh seo.

Sheall Raonaid air na cùirtearan a-rithist. 'Bidh mi air ais ann
an diog,' thuirt i gu h-obann agus choisich i a-steach dhan taigh
gu slaodach, gu cugallach.

Cho luath 's a chaidh i à sealladh, choimhead am balach timcheall air. Bha e am beachd teicheadh nuair a mhothaich e gun robh pram sa phoirdse. Rinn e gàire ris fhèin. Sin e – bha pàiste san taigh, ogha a' bhoireannaich 's dòcha. Cò nach gabhadh dragh mu dheidhinn bragan neo-àbhaisteach, is pàiste san taigh?

Sheas e an àirde. Seo a' chiad neach-ceannaich dham bruidhinn e ann an dha-rìribh agus cha robh e airson innse do Steaphan nach d' fhuair e fiù 's tron doras-aghaidh.

Thill Raonaid ann am priobadh na sùla, mus robh tìde aig a' bhalach coimhead tro na nòtaichean aige a-rithist. Cha robh a h-aodann cho glas no cho sgìth 's a bha e mus deach i a-steach dhan taigh. Smèid i ris a' bhalach.

'Nach tig thu a-steach?' thuirt i ris. 'Cuiridh mi air an coire agus faodaidh tu innse dhomh mu na barganan a th' agad.'

Chuala am balach guth Steaphain na cheann: *Ma gheibh thu cuireadh dol a-steach dhan taigh, faodaidh tu a bhith cinnteach às gum bi iad deònach* rudeigin *a cheannach bhuat. Na fàg an taigh gus an cuir iad ainm ri cùmhnant, fiù 's ma bhios tu ann fad na h-oidhche.*

Dh'fheuch e gun èisteachd ris a' ghuth eile na cheann, a bha ag ràdh nach robh còir aige dol faisg air an taigh.

Lean e Raonaid a-steach dhan trannsa. Cha b' ann a-steach dhan t-seòmar san robh na cùirtearan dùinte a chaidh i, ach a-steach dhan chidsin bheag, dhathach aig cùl an taighe. Bha treidhe air a' bhòrd ann am meadhan a' chidsin, air an robh briosgaidean, poit, ceithir cupannan agus botal do leanabh.

Thog Raonaid cupa eile bhon phreas agus lìon i e le tì bhon phoit.

'Bainne, siùcar?' dh'fhaighnich i, às dèidh dhi sèithear a tharraing a-mach dhan bhalach.

Chrom am balach a cheann agus shuidh e sìos.

'Briosgaid?' dh'fhaighnich i.

Chrath am balach a cheann. Bha fàileadh neònach san taigh, coltach ri bùth charthannais, agus bha e coltach gur ann bho bhùth charthannais a thàinig cuid de na briosgaidean cuideachd.

'Nis,' thuirt Raonaid, cho luath 's a bha i fhèin na suidhe aig
a' bhòrd, is briosgaid na làmh, 'nach innis thu dhomh mu na
h-uinneagan agad – dè tha cho sònraichte math mun deidhinn?'

Choimhead am balach timcheall air mus tuirt e facal. Carson a
bha an taigh cho sàmhach? Cha robh guth air na bragan a chuala
e na bu thràithe, no air pàiste. A bharrachd air na cupannan, cha
robh sgeul air duine eile.

Bha trì dealbhan air balla a' chidsin: Raonaid agus duine àrd air
latha am bainnse; Raonaid còmhla ris an aon duine, is bèibidh na
gàirdeanan; Raonaid, an duine agus balach mu cheithir bliadhna
a dh'aois air an tràigh. Bha e coltach gun deach na dealbhan a
thogail anns na 80an no 90an.

'Saoil . . . am bi an duine agaibh airson cluinntinn mu na
h-uinneagan cuideachd?' dh'fhaighnich e. 'No an còrr den
teaghlach?'

Dhùin Raonaid a sùilean airson diog no dhà agus, nuair a
dh'fhosgail i iad, rinn i fiamh-ghàire fhuadain. Choimhead ise
air na dealbhan cuideachd.

'Siud agad Ailean agus Chris, am balach beag againn. Uill, chan
e balach beag a th' ann tuilleadh – cha chreideadh tu e, ach tha e
fhèin pòsta a-nis, is bèibidh ùr aige fhèin is Eilidh. Olivia bheag –
chan eil i ach còig mìosan a dh'aois.'

Chuimhnich am balach air moladh eile bho Steaphan: *Gabh
ùidh annta. Ma tha iadsan a' leantainn ball-coise, tha thusa a' lean-
tainn ball-coise. Ma tha cù acasan, tha an aon seòrsa cù agad fhèin
no aig do mhàthair.*

Thog am balach fòn bhon bhaga, bhrùth e air an sgrion turas
no dhà agus sheall e do Raonaid e.

'Seallaibh seo, bha bèibidh aig mo phiuthar as sine o chionn
ceithir mìosan – 's e Olivia a chuir iad oirrese cuideachd.'

Air an sgrion, bha bèibidh bhrèagha, chruinn, le pluicean dearga,
na laighe ri taobh teadaidh a bha nas motha na i fhèin.

Cha tuirt Raonaid facal agus, nuair a choimhead am balach oirre,
ghabh e dragh gun rachadh i lag.

Dh'fhosgail i agus dhùin i a beul turas no dhà agus tharraing i anail mhòr, dhomhainn. Mu dheireadh thall, dh'innis i dhan bhalach ann an guth cugallach gun robh am fòn aice fhèin briste. Mura robh, thuirt i, bhiodh i air dealbhan den Olivia aice fhèin a shealltainn dha.

Rinn am balach fiamh-ghàire lag, chuir e am fòn air falbh agus thòisich e a bhruidhinn mu dheidhinn uinneagan a-rithist.

'Tha sinn a' tairgsinn bargan sònraichte an-diugh fhèin . . . '

'Ò!' dh'èigh Raonaid gu h-obann, mus robh cothrom aig a' bhalach dad eile a ràdh. 'Thà rudeigin agam ri shealltainn dhut!'

Leum i a-mach às a' chidsin agus thill i mus robh cothrom aig a' bhalach a sheacaid a chur air. Bha ailbhean bog na làmh – ailbhean a bha gorm aig aon àm, ach a bha glas is lom a-nis. Bha e follaiseach gun deach a shròn a tharraing dheth agus a chàradh turas no dhà.

'Seo Nelly,' thuirt Raonaid, is i a' cur an ailbhein ghroid air a' bhòrd air beulaibh a' bhalaich. 'B' ann le Chris a bha i, agus 's ann le Olivia a tha i a-nis.'

Gu slaodach, ghluais am balach an cupa is na pàipearan aige air falbh bho Nelly bhochd. Bha e soilleir nach deach a nighe a-riamh.

Shuidh Raonaid air ais aig a' bhòrd, thog i Nelly agus ghabh i boladh domhainn dhith. Lìon a sùilean le deòir.

Choimhead am balach air falbh bhuaipe. Cha do dh'obraich siud cho math 's a bha e an dùil. Bha e am beachd tilleadh dhan sgriobt aige nuair a chaidh aire a ghlacadh leis a' ghlas-chrochaidh mhòr air an doras-cùil. *Cuir an t-eagal orra*, bha Steaphan air a ràdh. *Ma chuireas tu teagamh nan inntinnean mu shàbhailteachd nan uinneagan aca, bidh iad ro thoilichte tèarainteachd a cheannach bhuat, aig prìs sam bith.*

Thog e catalog bhon bhaga agus thòisich e a' bruidhinn mu dheidhinn tèarainteachd.

'Mar a chì sibh,' thuirt e, 'tha na h-uinneagan seo air duaisean a ghlèidheadh – chan fhaigh thu uinneagan cho sàbhailte bho bhuidheann sam bith eile. Nach eil iad a' coimhead snog cuideachd – tha stoidhle againn a dh'fhreagras air a h-uile taigh, is a h-uile teaghlach. Ma tha Olivia bheag gu bhith an seo gu tric, nach eil sibh airson 's gum bi an taigh cho sàbhailte 's a ghabhas? Seallaibh seo, bidh sinn a' cur glasan sònraichte air a h-uile uinneag.'

Bha e air aire Raonaid a ghlacadh a-rithist. Sheas i, is Nelly fhathast na làmhan, agus choimhead i sìos air. Bha fearg na sùilean.

'Tha an teaghlach agamsa sàbhailte gu leòr – cò dh'innis dhut nach eil? Bidh mise a' dèanamh cinnteach nach tèid cron sam bith a dhèanamh orra, nach tig duine sam bith faisg orra. Tha iad uile an seo, còmhla rium, agus bidh iad còmhla rium a-chaoidh. Uile còmhla, uile sàbhailte, mar bu chòir.'

Sheas am balach cuideachd agus thòisich e a' sgioblachadh an stuth aige. On a nochd e aig doras an taighe, bha e air a bhith nearbhasach, mì-chofhurtail agus fiù 's draghail, ach a-nis cha robh e ach seachd searbh sgìth den deamhnaidh obair seo. A' chiad latha aige, a' chiad taigh dhan deach e, agus cò bha ga fheitheamh? Cailleach chraicte.

Choimhead e air an uaireadair, chuir e cairt sìos air a' bhòrd agus thuirt e gun robh coinneamh eile aige air taobh eile a' bhaile.

Cha tuirt Raonaid facal.

'Math ur coinneachadh,' thuirt e nuair a ràinig e an doras, 'cuiribh fios dhan oifis ma tha sibh . . . no an duine agaibh airson barrachd a chluinntinn mu na h-uinneagan.'

Bha an taigh fhathast cho sàmhach ris an uaigh.

Dhùin Raonaid an doras air a cùlaibh agus thill i dhan chidsin, far an do lìon i ceithir cupannan agus botal dhan teaghlach aice.

*

Leth-uair a thìde às dèidh dha taigh Raonaid fhàgail, bha am balach na sheasamh ann an seòmar-suidhe air taobh eile na sràide. Fhad 's a bha e a' bruidhinn ri Anna is Iain, nàbaidhean Raonaid, mu dheidhinn uinneagan trì-ghlainneach, ruith nighean bheag a-steach dhan t-seòmar.

'Fuirich mionaid, Olivia,' thuirt Anna, 'tha sinn a' bruidhinn ris an duine seo an-dràsta – nach dèan thu dealbh sa chidsin gus am bi sinn deiseil? Tha pàipear is peansailean air a' bhòrd.'

Dh'fhalbh an nighean a-rithist, is bus oirre.

'Nach eil sin snog,' thuirt am balach, a bha a' faireachdainn nas misneachail san taigh àbhaisteach seo, far an robh cothrom aige an sgriobt a leantainn. 'Olivia agaibh an seo agus Olivia bheag air taobh eile na sràide.'

Sheall Anna is Iain air a chèile. 'Olivia air taobh eile na sràide?' dh'fhaighnich Iain le iongnadh na ghuth. 'Chan eil pàiste sam bith san taigh siud. Nach do . . . '

Chuir Anna a làmh air a ghàirdean. 'Iain,' thuirt i gu sàmhach.

Leig am balach osna às. Dè bha ceàrr air muinntir na sràide seo? Cha robh gin de na dòighean-reic aig Steaphan ag obair dha an seo.

'Cha robh nighean san taigh, an robh?' dh'fhaighnich Anna, is rudeigin coltach ri eagal na guth.

'Chan fhaca mi i,' thuirt am balach, a' faireachdainn mì-chofhurtail a-rithist, 'ach bha an teaghlach uile san ath sheòmar . . . Chris, an e? Is a bhean, Eilidh, agus Olivia, am bèibidh ùr.'

Sheall Anna a-mach às an uinneag airson deagh ghreis.

''S dòcha nach eil còir agam innse dhut,' thuirt i, gun choimhead air Iain, 'ach cha robh duine sam bith ann. Bhàsaich iad.'

'Dè?' thuirt am balach. Choimhead e timcheall air – bha e air gu leòr a chluinntinn mu na cleasan a chluicheadh iad air luchd-obrach air a' chiad latha aca. An robh Steaphan falaichte anns a' bhana siud aig bonn na sràide? An robh camara ann an taigh Raonaid, agus san taigh seo? An robh iad uile a' coimhead air san oifis is a' magadh air?

'Bhàsaich Ailean, duine Raonaid, agus Chris, am mac, o chionn deich bliadhna fichead,' thuirt Anna. 'Bha iad air saor-làithean agus thuit Chris a-steach dhan abhainn. Leum Ailean a-steach airson a shàbhaladh, ach bha an sruth ro làidir agus chaidh an dithis aca a bhàthadh. Cha robh Raonaid a-riamh mar a bha i ron tubaist – 's beag an t-iongnadh. Cha robh for agam gun robh i fhathast a' leigeil oirre gun robh Ailean is Chris beò ge-tà. Bhiodh Chris air a bhith trithead 's a còig am bliadhna – feumaidh gun do chruthaich i bean is pàiste dha na h-inntinn.'

Bha sùilean Anna làn deòir agus chuir Iain a ghàirdean timcheall oirre.

'Saoil a bheil còir againn fios a chur gu Màiri, a piuthar?' dh'fhaighnich e. 'Nach do dh'fhàg i àireamh-fòn an seo dhuinn?'

Bhris am balach a-steach air. 'Ach bha *cuideigin* eile ann – chuala mi fuaimean anns an taigh fhad 's a bha mi a' bruidhinn rithe air an stairsnich.'

Bha e air co-dhùnadh a ruighinn – seo an latha mu dheireadh aige san obair seo. Cha tilleadh e dhan oifis agus chuireadh e fòn gu Marc madainn a-màireach, feuch an robh obair fhathast ri fhaighinn sa bhùth spòrs. Ged nach biodh an tuarastal cho math, cha bhiodh aige ri dèiligeadh ri bàs, bròn no bèibidhean nach robh ann.

'Cò aig a tha fios dè dhèanadh fuaim,' bha Iain ag ràdh, 'ach chan eil duine sam bith san taigh ud ach Raonaid bhochd. Chan eil ann ach taibhsean.'

Cha robh ùidh sam bith aig a' bhalach ann an uinneagan tuilleadh. Dh'fhaodadh Steaphan fhèin tilleadh dhan deamhnaidh sràid seo agus barganan fuadain a thairgsinn dhaibh nan togradh e.

Rinn am balach leisgeul agus dh'fhàg e taigh Anna is Iain cho luath 's a b' urrainn dha. Air an t-slighe air ais dhan stèisean, thilg e na pàipearan aige dhan bhiona.

*

Air taobh eile na sràide, bha Raonaid agus a teaghlach a' coimhead air *Bargain Hunt*, is trì cupannan teatha a' fuarachadh air am beulaibh. Choimhead i orra le pròis. Ged a bha Ailean air tuiteam far na sòfa na bu thràithe, bha e cofhurtail a-nis.

B' ann o chionn deich bliadhna a bha Raonaid air Ailean is Chris a lorg, taobh a-muigh bùtha sa bhaile a bha air cuidhteas fhaighinn de na seann *mannequins* aca. Bha an dithis aca nan laighe aig doras-cùil na bùtha agus cha b' urrainn do Raonaid coiseachd seachad orra.

O chionn còig bliadhna, bha a' bhùth air boireannach a bha air aon chas a chall a thilgeil a-mach – Eilidh. Gu fortanach, bha i fhèin agus Chris uabhasach measail air a chèile agus phòs iad goirid às dèidh sin. Bha Raonaid ro thoilichte an dreasa-bainnse aice fhèin a chur air Eilidh agus deiseachan ùra a cheannach do dh'Ailean is Chris.

Choimhead Raonaid sìos air Olivia na gàirdeanan agus rinn i gàire. Cha robh duine air Olivia a thilgeil a-mach – bha ise air a bhith na pàirt de thaisbeanadh anns a' bhùth aig àm na Nollaig. Màthair, athair agus bèibidh, is geansaidhean Nollaig orra uile. Leig Raonaid oirre gun robh i a' faireachdainn tinn agus, fhad 's a bha luchd-obrach na bùtha a' faighinn glainne uisge is sèithear dhi, ghoid i Olivia bhon taisbeanadh agus chuir i am bèibidh gu faiceallach aig bonn a' bhaga aice.

'Bèibidh na Nollaig,' thuirt i ri Chris is Eilidh nuair a thill i dhachaigh. B' e sin an Nollaig a b' fheàrr a bh' aig an teaghlach a-riamh.

Nuair a thàinig *Bargain Hunt* gu crìoch, sheas i agus thug i sùil tro na cùirtearan. Bha e coltach gun robh sròn Anna, an nàbaidh aice, a' cur dragh oirre a-rithist. Bha i fhèin, Iain agus am balach nearbhasach siud a' coimhead air taigh Raonaid agus a' coimhead muladach.

Dhùin Raonaid na cùirtearan a-rithist, chuir i Olivia sìos air an t-sòfa eadar Eilidh agus Chris agus thug i pòg do dh'Ailean.

'Nis,' thuirt i, 'seallaibh air an uair – an dèan mi ceapairean dhuibh uile mus tòisich *Cash in the Attic*?'

Thog i na cupannan agus choisich i air ais dhan chidsin, a' seinn tàladh fo a h-anail, airson biadh is teatha a dhèanamh dhan teaghlach aice.

Rachel Carmichael
EVERY REVOLUTION HAS ITS CASUALTIES

She was often sent to the goods yard to retrieve smokers. The tannoy couldn't be heard there – nobody had a mobile phone then – and Teresa the supervisor was on her feet all day every day, so Lorna had to do it. She walked along the aisles – today she chose pet food and cleaning products, nothing to make her hungry – past the bakery counter, the fish counter, through to the back shop and the stale fat and sweat odours of the canteen and staff changing rooms, then outside to the grey tarmac ringed with metal fencing. She readied herself for the reaction when she turned up to interrupt a quiet smoke and chat, or a flirtation with the HGV drivers. One of the older men from the bakery saw her first.

God almighty, I've been here two minutes.

It's Carey I'm looking for, Lorna said.

He didn't apologise.

She found Carey leaning against a tree, eyes closed and face tilted to the sun. Lorna didn't remember seeing a tree in the yard before. It was in bloom – a cherry tree. Unmissable really.

Supervisor's looking for you, Lorna said.

Carey took a long draw and offered what was left to Lorna, who declined.

I didn't think you would, Carey said. You're on the front desk. Nice voice for announcements.

She crushed her cigarette into a tree root and held out a hand. Lorna helped her up. Tall like she was, a year younger at eighteen. Lorna had seen Carey at break times, when they coincided. The supermarket's gingham polyester looked good on her.

Carey brushed dust and pink petals off the backs of her legs.

Is my arse okay? she said.

There's some in your hair.

Carey tilted her head for Lorna to brush them off.

Better get back before Teresa has a stroke, Carey said. I shouldn't say that, you know what happened to her mother. She can't have not told you. Martyr Teresa. You know she still lives with her parents? They're up the road from us. Sad case.

They walked back to the shop floor together. Carey talking, Lorna learning things she didn't know about the staff, the managers, some of the customers – things she would never have guessed. Lorna found a petal sticking to her sleeve when she changed to go home, and she remembered the tree.

At other times in her life, she thought about that day, and how Carey's presence drew your attention to things, made them seem more interesting because of their proximity to her.

*

There are some thoughts a decent person should not have. Lorna believes this, even while having those thoughts. The twins have an away match on Saturday, thank you God. Brandon's mother will drive them there and back – and expects no one to return the favour. A good parent – a working parent – would not admit to the exhilaration of the freed time, the gift of six weekend hours.

Lorna blows a kiss to the boys from the window, already thinking about what to wear to brunch at Anna's. They started talking one Saturday in the rugby clubhouse, the weekend Brandon's mother was in hospital. The other parents were outside in the rain, standing by the touchline. Anna was there when Lorna arrived, her head bowed over a paperback, her clothes drawing Lorna's attention. That silk shirt in a shade of yellow only Anna's frequent holidays let her get away with. Lorna wondered about her age. They say women become invisible at forty-two. She couldn't imagine that happening to Anna.

In her bedroom Lorna's hand flicks through the clothes on the rails of her wardrobe, dismissing her yellow cotton, settling for black.

She had assumed Anna would not want anything to do with her. Lorna used to work in Anna's husband's firm and knew that Anna had stopped work after their second baby. But after the rugby match came an invitation to coffee, reciprocated, then a series of lunches that at first felt to Lorna like obligations.

She turns on the dishwasher and hangs up some washing, thinking of the load that will come home later. Anna, she realises, is the person from the boys' school who she knows best. The person to whom she tells the most – but not everything. Anna, with her twice-weekly gardener and housekeeper Mondays to Fridays, her familiarity with exams and university rankings and rugby camps. She is unsure why she keeps up the friendship – she supposes that is now what it is. She knows she is shallow enough to enjoy seeing inside Anna's house, and the clothes she chooses to wear, but tells herself these are part of her own education. Besides, Anna has information about the school and the teachers, she knows what's coming because her older daughter has been through it all. And unusually among the parent group, Anna isn't always nice.

Outside Anna's house Lorna unmutes her phone. The bland ringtone she thought unintrusive now reminds her of work, and triggers a pain in her stomach, but it would not do to miss an emergency message from the coach. There is a missed call from her mother. It isn't the agreed day for their conversation – Lorna has had to be strict about that. She knows it will be something unimportant and depressing, the usual news from a small town. Someone's illness, or expected demise.

There's also a text.

Did you hear about Carey?

And a second one, her mother unable to wait for a reply.

Passed away aged forty-one. I'll find out more.

*

There's a chair in the hallway of Anna's house, near the front door. Lorna knows there is another one on the landing halfway up the stairs, and one in the main bathroom. She's had the tour. Their purpose seems to be to draw attention to the fact that the house is big enough to accommodate them. Lorna has brought flowers from the florist's in Anna's neighbourhood.

Anna arranges food onto plates, a rough linen apron with leather straps protecting her clothes. She is commanding at the marble island, reaching confidently for everything she wants, without having to search. As Anna talks, Lorna sees Carey back when they worked together, reaching behind to the right spot on the right shelf for the cigarettes the customer asked for, not having to look. She wonders whether she herself has ever looked so competent.

Everything okay? Anna is looking at her.

Lorna has been holding her fork for too long. She dislikes hot and cold on the same plate, scrambled eggs straight from the pan and avocado out of the fridge. But only an ingrate would complain.

Delicious, she says.

She remembers things Carey told her, trivial things that she is surprised not to have forgotten. How mouldy lemon was the worst smell in the world, no debate. The names she made up for the store manager and poor Teresa. The time she came to work with a scarf tied round her head, like the one Madonna wore in a film. Teresa objected. But Carey said her hair was unmanageable.

Every hairdresser I've been to says the same. This is the most hygienic option.

It isn't part of the uniform, Teresa said. But her shoulders were already drooping.

There's nothing I can do, said Carey, bringing the matter to a conclusion. I didn't see you at Mass, Teresa. Is your mum okay?

And Teresa's eyes would soften and gleam in her hard face.

How many times had Lorna remembered this, and thought of Carey? How many times, for all that time, and she never tried to make contact.

How's Ewan? How long is he away for this time, Anna is asking.

Three more weeks.

You're okay with it now?

Sure, Lorna said. There's not much chance to misbehave in the North Sea.

She had practised this response. People didn't think about the night onshore before the flight home. Or if they did, they didn't say.

*

Teresa moved Carey from the checkouts to the info desk. Lorna looked forward to explaining how things were done.

I'll figure it out, Carey said. She rested her hands on the counter, drummed her fingers. I'm going to finish with Ian tonight. I don't want to meet his parents. He's a right boring bastard.

Lorna tried to look as if she agreed on this course of action. She'd never heard of Ian.

The manager decided that the Saturday staff should carry out the weekly tobacco stocktake, until further notice. Either Carey or Lorna would have to go to the warehouse and count every box and case of cigarettes, cigars and tobacco. They were stacked high on shelves, several rows deep. Carey said it was fingernail-breaking work.

The manager doesn't trust the full-timers. They're all shagging the guys from the butcher department.

Teresa decided Lorna should do it.

The tobacco products were in a corner of the warehouse enclosed by metal fencing, in the style of a cage. The key to the little door built into the front had to be collected from and returned to the deputy manager, signed in and out. The first half hour was what Lorna hated, the quantity of boxes and packets daunting and the cage left untidy by the full-timers, and always, as she made her way through the clear Perspex curtain between the shop floor and the warehouse, one of the butchers would call out and ask her to slip him twenty Bensons and his colleagues would laugh. But she soon got absorbed in what she had to do and found it easy to give herself to the task, working through it till her hands were grey with dust, and the mess and chaos had been turned into neat lists of numbers. Some days she could think about other things as she counted, let daydreams take over her mind, of good things that might happen to her.

One Saturday Carey surprised her.

I'll do the stocktake today. You've done it for months, it's taking the piss.

I don't mind it, Lorna said.

She liked to get away from people for a couple of hours. People looking at her, asking questions, returning things they weren't happy with. But Carey was already on her way.

Just before the end of third lunch, and Lorna losing her chance to go for hot food, Carey came running towards the desk, giving an impression that her whole morning had been conducted at speed. She asked Lorna to check her calculations. Her totals were different every time. She stood close to Lorna, holding the clipboard and following the columns of figures with her pen as Lorna put numbers in the calculator.

There was a mark on the front of Carey's uniform.

You've got something on you.

Shit. Carey snorted. You don't want to know what that is.

Lorna kept her arms tight by her sides.

You know Stephen on the deli counter? Carey said.

Quiet, athletic Stephen, who talked to Lorna sometimes about music and football, and joining the TA. Of course, Stephen.

God, he's amazing, Carey said.

*

Anna talks a lot about her husband, dull details about his career, in exchange for which Lorna offers modest snippets about her own.

Lorna pictures Fraser as Anna speaks, the features that huddle together in the centre of his pale face, and she remembers the fruit scones her mother used to serve up – all the sultanas clustered at the bottom – before giving up baking for good. A mean look to Fraser's face, she always thought, though Lorna has seen no evidence of actual meanness from either of the couple. They are generous people, if at times grasping. When Lorna told Anna they were upgrading their barbecue Anna didn't hesitate.

We'll have the old one, for the cottage.

It wasn't a question, there was no please. It would never occur to Anna that Lorna might know people who couldn't buy their own.

There is fruit salad after the eggs and avocado. Straight from the fridge, the strawberries flavourless.

Lorna conducts conversational experiments. In response to Anna's family achievements she talks about her niece's struggles at her mediocre school. Her nephew being suspended for the third and final time. To Anna the other family's pain does not register, they are too different. Lorna may as well be talking about a puppy's separation anxiety.

Carey would have mimicked both of them, she could do anyone's voice. Taken the piss out of Lorna and Anna, their poise, their tact and polite language. The obscene handbags and the sparkling circles of metal they both wear, to indicate something or other.

Lorna? Anna's speaking again, looking more directly at her now.

Sorry Anna. Lorna raises her dessert spoon. This is all lovely.

You're miles away today.

My mum just called.

Did somebody die?

Something like that, Lorna shrugs.

I was talking about Fraser. He's been getting home after midnight, a lot. Eleven times this month, to be exact.

Business must be good.

Do you have to do that? It must be exhausting.

It's the culture of his firm. It can be that way sometimes, Lorna
says. I wouldn't worry.

No. I just wondered if you have to do that too.

*

Lorna considered taking up smoking, so she wouldn't get hungry
and have to go to the canteen and eat fry-ups with people who
hated students. She never saw Carey eat anything other than the
wine gums and fruit pastilles she stowed in the pockets of her
uniform. To keep her going, she said. And sometimes she would
hold packets of pipe tobacco to her nose and inhale. It wasn't that
Carey was very thin, although she was as slim as anyone would
want to be: her proportions were right. What Lorna's mother
would call well put-together. One of the phrases she never applied
to her own daughter.

Saturdays began to feel longer. Carey was taking longer to do
the stocktake. They had little time to speak, and Carey had less to
tell now that Stephen was the only one she was seeing.

Still, any resentment lifted, Lorna could only feel pleasure when
she heard the fresh produce boys whistling and looked round to
see Carey on her way back from the warehouse, rosy and smiling.
Lorna worried how she looked, standing next to Carey behind
the counter. Carey had once assured her, after a disappointment
at the student union, that they only put good-looking ones on
the front desk. Even the full-timers, she said, if you look past
their shit makeup.

Stephen wants to see this crappy band tonight, Carey said. He
got tickets without asking me.

Lorna had heard him talk about their new album.

They're good, you'll enjoy it.

I don't think I can stand it. I went to that place before – nobody
dances, they just stand with their hands in their pockets. Appreciating
the music.

Lorna laughed as Carey demonstrated.

You go, Carey said. Saturday night, you can't be studying.

My first exam's on Monday.

Carey took hold of her arms.

Please Lorna, I can't be arsed. You like that stuff, he's told me. He likes you.

Lorna thought about what she still had to do, the lectures she'd been putting off re-reading and revising. A customer came, there was a refund to process, and she filled in the form and thought about how it would feel to share an experience with someone like Stephen, to see this band they both liked. It would be her first time at a gig in the city. Something long overdue, like so many other things. She'd be talking to him all night between songs, standing next to him in the near-dark, with a drink – what would she have to drink? What did Carey drink? – she could have something similar but not the same. And what to wear? There was no time to go shopping, and little money anyway. She could joke with him, gently, about Carey's taste in music and they'd understand each other. But maybe Carey didn't mean it.

Are you serious? What time does it start?

Aw, I'll go with him, keep him happy, Carey said. I know I'm lucky. When you've finished those exams we're going out and getting blootered and I'm finding you a man.

Lorna consoled herself, imagining a night out with Carey. But maybe Carey didn't mean that either.

*

Teresa had questions.

When did Carey start going to the warehouse? How long does she take there, do you have to help her?

It had been a busy morning. A group of pensioners came in for a supply of cigarettes to see them through a fishing trip, there were four returns from a bad batch of jam doughnuts, then a woman in a camel coat and gold jewellery argued at length that she should be able to use fifteen discount coupons against the purchase of one packet of Superkings.

I think maybe Stephen helps her, Lorna said.

Is that so?

When Teresa came back to the desk, Carey was with her.

You do today's stocktake again. From scratch. Carey's staying put, she doesn't need a tea break.

When Lorna was finished, Carey told her that Teresa had walked into the tobacco cage and found Stephen lying on the floor.

I had to go to the bathroom. We were going to leave, he was just waiting for me, then she turns up. Why didn't she send you? Why didn't you say you'd get me?

Lorna fumbled with the pages in the clipboard, looking for something her eyes could fix on, hoping that Teresa hadn't said too much.

She gave me a written warning, the cow. Stephen was going to quit anyway.

*

In her mind Lorna runs through possible causes of death. Things Carey talked about, family illnesses. She always had stories of men – boys, as they were then. Lorna with so little to offer in return, Carey not making a thing of it. Funny how they'd got on so well. If they'd been at the same school they wouldn't have.

There are no photographs. Back then you wouldn't take a camera to mundane places like work. Nor does Lorna know Carey's last name now, the name she died with. She hopes she didn't change it. What an effort it used to be, to stay in touch. And how difficult now not to. Impossible almost, to lose touch without losing face – even with the loosest connections. Every one of them, appearing everywhere, waiting to be liked. Anna, the only exception.

Lorna decides on a cancer, cervical most likely. Imagines Carey overweight but still attractive. Glamorous. Divorced at least once.

*

Lorna answers her mother's call.

A motorbike accident in Vietnam, she says, not asking how Lorna and the boys are. Apparently they did all sorts, she and Stephen. Munros too, and kite-surfing, I think that's what it's called. All over the world, after they left the army. At least she packed a lot in, poor girl.

When's the funeral?

Are you planning to go? Her mother is quiet for a second. I hope you've not been dwelling on things.

*

Stephen doesn't recognise her when she shakes his hand, and Lorna doesn't offer her name. In middle age he looks ordinary. Perhaps he always did.

Outside the crematorium she approaches a woman whose face is familiar. The woman peers at her.

I'm Lorna. I used to work on the front desk with Carey. At weekends.

Teresa's hair is a different colour, but she still has the same watery blue eyeliner and navy mascara.

I'm from here. I was a student back then, I moved away after uni.

It's awfully good of you to come, Teresa says. To remember her. She looks over Lorna's shoulder.

Her poor parents, Teresa says. She was still the baby of the family. And she was a one-off, Carey was, no-one would forget her. You can see that. She tilts her head to the crowd, and touches Lorna's arm before she walks away.

Many of them look like they're not from the town, the clothes and jewellery too exuberant somehow, their movements unself-conscious. And the others, the ones she might once have known, don't recognise Lorna. Has she changed so much, she wonders, or did nobody ever see her. Two small children – they can't be Carey's – are playing on the steps, unreprimanded. A group of elderly women stand in a circle, one of them telling the others about Vietnam's excellent hospitals. The celebrant is smiling into the middle distance, her job done.

Lorna will not go to the reception.

Leonie Charlton
OPAL

(twenty-four years)

Luing cattle follow you, bellowing their brindles and sheer reds up a hillside. The bull heaves: flanks measuring the gravity of each step. Muzzles run with love and cows call throat-water sounds. Hooves sink and bones lever this whole of hide and milk and muscle. Calves gather, surge forwards, light in their eyes and feet. In a lull things happen: the bull raises his head and lets pheromones pour across his gums; calves throw their weight at udders, come up white-mouthed, frothing. Behind all this the air is raucous with trodden bog myrtle, fresh cow shit, sunshine. Clegs bite. I swat my skin, breathe it all in. I remember, effortfully, before I forget –

> that way you look back at your cows
> how your t-shirt pins your clavicles
> makes me want to start all over

MRS MACLEAN

Her memory is mostly updraft, embering
eighty-three years of nature's gleanings –
like knowing-fine
that October's nettles are the fiercest

last night a toad circled the house
he poisoned her sense of home
and today she misplaced a whole turnip
has looked in all the obvious old places

is still looking now by brittle moonlight
keeping a beady eye out for drag-marks
and toe-dabs of a predating toad,
the coppered stare and deft tongue.
Her memory is mostly updraft, embering.

F. E. Clark
O'KEEFFE, LIKE A BELL

Georgia O'Keeffe fell from the glass covering the framed 3-D map of the Cairngorms, hanging above the cold studio radiator. It was a grey Monday morning, the world was in free fall, burning and bloated, a tricky new moon in Virgo fucking up my days. A keepsake from an exhibition of her work at the Tate Modern – in black and white O'Keeffe is posing, head to one side, arms framing her profile. She might be naked, it's not clear. The weight of the postcard had finally beaten the white-blue tack, leaving skid marks down the glass, in the sky above Mount Keen and Glen Tanar. O'Keeffe settled, her perfect curved ear just showing, wedged into the top of the radiator beneath Granton-on-Spey. When she fell, she clanged, striking the metal like a bell – wake up! Wake the fuck up, she pealed.

Alison Cohen

TOWARDS A DEFINITION OF DAUGHTER

Hate is expressed by the existence of the end of the 'hour'.
(D. W. Winnicott, 'Hate in the Countertransference', *Collected Papers*,
p. 197)

Years ago, I told a friend *my father is dementing*
and she said I must expect to put my life on hold.

    And just before my mother died
    I told her not to worry, I'd take care of Dad –
    was all possessiveness,
    pleased they'd made me sole attorney.

Last month I told a poet *my father is dementing*
and she said she'd never heard dementing used as a
                verb before.

    It's 'Daisy, Daisy' –
    a slowing, slurring Hal

Yesterday I told a neighbour *my father is dementing*
and she said *shame!*

    It isn't what she meant but I am ashamed –

    today I talked to him about his carer's leave
    and, without a clue how many lives he's using up

    he said with warm affection *she doesn't need a break* –
    I laughed a laugh of cruel holes –

    and he looked at me on our video call
    a look that was all confusion, trust and asking, muddled up.

ON THE LACK OF A HORSE

He's asking for his memory, is upset –
his reason's somewhere in this house
but he can't find it.

Of course, he says *we don't have a horse just now,*
his *just now* making me almost laugh out loud –
as if we'd ever had a horse.

I search this still familiar field, half-abandoned
by his bolting mind – find he's needing horsehair
in place of neural pathways, to hang again

the garden mobile, battered down by storms –
Oh, let it scatter light again,
please him.

As a student I was told
It's easy for the patient, he's oblivious
but there's a lot of brain before you're down to basics –

he's peeing on the kitchen floor,
is like a horse with blinkers
seeing just a narrow stable, frightened by the rest.

Aged six I'd begged him
Dad, please, let me take her home –
Bernadette, who drew our caravan that week,

knew her way around the lanes of Mayo,
was nuzzling and comfort
was old herself, being sent to pasture –

I couldn't understand his saying no.
Now he thinks he bought her
and she's gone.

Lucy Cunningham
SWEDISH FISH

A cried when Da telt me that the fishes that swam in the pond were the same type of fishes we ate fir supper on Fridays. A always liked watching the trouts, waiting fir them tae bump against the bank and somersault around like circus ladies wi scales. A'd take some crumbs or whatever a had oot ma pocket, and throw them in the water when they did that. Loaf-ends, gummies and sometimes even sweetie wrappers. But they'd eat whatever it wis wioot fussing like a always did at tea time and quickly they'd see where the upside wis and stop splashing around all confused.

'Ye canny dae that, son,' Da said tae me one afternoon when a wis slipping gummies intae the pond.

'Dae wit Da?' He'd jist laughed at me like adults always dae wioot telling me wit the joke wis.

'Ye cannae feed them Swedish fish pal. It seems a bit wrong, don't ye think?' Wee fishes, the same size as the red, chewy, Swedish ones were munching the sweeties whole and doubling in size and ma belly got sore jist thinking aboot it. 'Wee fishes eating other wee fishes . . . a mean, would ye eat a wee boy if a fed you one?' A fished some of the sweeties oot of the water.

'Dinnae wiste that sweetie, son,' he said tae me, taking it oot ma hand and wiping it doon on his jeans. 'Well, it's jist as well ye didnae have a fish supper in yer pocket.'

A asked wit he meant and that's when he telt me aboot the pond fishes being the same as dinner fishes and a cried all the way home while he bit the heeds aff of them.

Ye'd think it would have been obvious, them having the same name and all. But they looked so different – those slimy wee things that danced aboot and munched on ma sweets in their rainbow coats and the pink, flaky thing that sat next tae ma peas and chips. A'd wondered if ma feeding them all those crumbs made them choke and die and infected them, breading their organs first and then eventually spreading tae the ootside, wrapping around their faces, preparing them fir the pan. But Da telt me that other folk dae the killing and that it wis normal. Wee fish get killed. Jist no by me. A jist eat them and feed them and watch them dae flips in the pond after school. A didnae feed them Swedish fish after that though, and a didnae visit the pond anymare on Fridays either.

*

When a grew up and turned seven, we didnae have fish and chips and peas much anymare and Da gave me a dug. Da had a bad leg and said he couldnae keep up wae me in the park but wee Clyde the dug could. In fact, a found it hard keeping up wae her sometimes. A'd throw her a stick or a wee chunk fae ma breakfast and she'd go bonkers and a swore she could be in the Olympics if that wis a thing fir dugs. A qualified fir ma school track team cos a had fast wee legs. A hated when Da said that. A wisnae that wee, jist oot of ma class a wis the weest. Da sent me oot wi Clyde fir training which wis jist a posh word fir playing in the park. A could run dead fast, tae be fair, especially when a wis having a good time and jist playing wi the dug. She wis getting fair fat but she still ran like a bullet.

A had a big race coming up and there wis a big hamper packed wi sweeties and biscuits fir the winner. Coach said that a could win it cos all the other lads were feart of me. A didnae ken why though cos a wis jist a wee thing wae no much meat on ma bones. A wisnae scary. A wis mare feart of the other lads. Ma mate Jim said they were scared because of wit folk said aboot ma da. They were always saying mad things aboot him but a didnae listen much cos Da telt me not tae. Coach got real close tae me and told me 'Jist make sure yer scaring them stiff and no making them leg it faster fae fright.' And there wis me, trembling fae the scrawny ankles up, worrying aboot how no tae scare folk. Coach gave ma hair a ruffle, unsticking it fae ma heed and a jist wanted ma dug.

On the day of the big race, a woke up shaking that bad the springs in ma mattress were pinging oot and skelping me. Da made me a big breakfast wi bacon rashers and eggs. It wis the best breakfast ever cos a wis sick tae death of porridge and a wis always fussing over it. But Da said old Wendy fae doon the road had sent the breakfast fir ma race day cos she saw how fast a'd been running oot the back field and how hard a'd been 'training'. A liked Wendy, especially her sultana scones when there werenae sultanas in them. She wis always in a wee pinnie wi cupcakes on it, peeking oot her kitchen window and mixing something. She shouted me over sometimes, tossed me a few scones and gave me a wee pinch on the cheek like old ladies always dae.

A ate up all of Wendy's bacon and eggs – a didnae know a plate could hold so much – and Da ate some porridge. A didnae even like the thought of the stuff in his mouth. Ma belly wisnae rumbling anymare but ma legs were still trembling wae the nerves. Da sent me oot and afore a walked aff tae school telt me that he thought a could win. He didnae say anything aboot it being because the other lads were scared of me, he jist thought a could win it. After that, a thought, a'd better win. The thing wis, a always ran faster when a wis having fun oot the back wi ma dug. So a hid around the corner until Da went tae his room or the cupboard then nipped back in tae get her. Da didnae walk me tae school like the other das did. He didnae leave the house much because when he did he grew a bad limp as if the door frame shot lasers that made his bones split or something. Wendy didnae answer the door when a went tae hers tae get ma tie done and ma hair slicked wi margarine like usual. A remember that part the most.

*

When the school bell rang, a went ootside tae get Clyde where a'd tied her leash tae the bike rack. All the girls wanted tae gie her a wee pet and squeaked aboot how she wis so chubby and so cute.

Everything wis cute tae them. Glittery pencil cases, hair clips, old fogeys dishing oot breath mints. Jist no me. They didnae find me cute. They were a bit feart of me. A untied the leash and walked wae Clyde and Jim up tae the stadium where the race wis. Ma legs were still a bit wobbly but the dug calmed me doon. A ruffled her hair. She wis panting like nothing else but a didnae have time tae get her water afore the race started. It wis a hot day and a felt bad fir leaving her oot there wioot anything tae drink. But a couldnae be thinking like that. A had tae think aboot how tae be scary, but no so scary that the boys sprinted faster. A had tae think aboot winning and making ma da and old Wendy proud. Da really liked sweeties and biscuits.

A got tae the starting line and some of the boys were whispering things. It wis maybe aboot me having ma dug wi me fir the race or maybe it wis aboot ma da. People were always saying mad things aboot ma da. They were always calling him mad. Saying things that wernae true. We got intae the starting position in a big line and that's when a realised Clyde wis flat on the ground and panting even heavier than afore. They shot the gun and the other lads sprinted aff, all gallus, some of them shooting their eyes back at me as they went. A spat on the ground, trying tae get her tae drink something but she wisnae having it. That's when a realised she wisnae thirsty, she wis having babies. It looked like the asphalt wis melting but a think it wis blood. But then again, it looked a bit like jam. A cannae be sure wit it wis.

*

A came back tae the house wi ma mucky running shoes in one plastic bag and three wee baby dugs in the other. A didnae even care aboot losing the race because Da would be so excited aboot the pups that he'd be proud of me anyway. A'd line us up and he'd ruffle all our heeds, one by one. But when a went inside Da wis crying intae the floor. He wis even kneeling on his bad knee.

'Wit's the matter Da? It's fine, a took Clyde tae school the day. She's no missing or anything.' A sat the puppies doon on the table and tried tae gie him a wee hug.

'Wendy died, pal. She had a heart attack this morning.'

A couldnae believe it. A looked oot the window and saw an ambulance and men lifting a big bin bag intae the back of it. There wis a few folk ootside crying. A didnae even think that Wendy might have a family. Old ladies always seem tae exist in ones.

'She wis really old Da. No like Ma wis. Doesnae that happen tae old people?'

'Aye it does, son.' He said.

'Then wit's the matter?'

Da sat up a wee bit and wiped his eyes aff. 'A guess a'll jist really miss her scones, pal. That's all.' A hadnae thought aboot that and then a felt like crying too.

A thought a might cheer Da up a wee bit by showing him the pups so a went and grabbed the carrier bag. 'A'm sorry Da, a didnae win the race the day, but look here.'

A shot a look at Da, excited tae see his big teeth appear and tae hear him laugh, but when a did he wis crying his eyes oot again. 'Wit's the matter now, Da? Don't ye like the wee pups?' He started walking up the stairs and heading tae the bedroom or the bath. Or maybe tae Ma's craft cupboard that he didnae open much cos all the kites and ribbons and pipe-cleaners came tiding oot ontae the linoleum. Ma belly got sore and ma legs started shaking again. A went tae ma room and took Clyde and the pups there, making sure they stayed away fae the burst springs on ma mattress and then went tae get them some supper. The fridge and the cupboards were empty, there wisnae even porridge. There wis only one tin of beans. A took them and popped the tin open on a spring and sat it doon fir the dugs. It wis dumb but a didnae know then that babies only drank their ma's milk fir a while when they're wee.

*

Da must have gone downstairs again cos the next time a heard him he wis yelling fae the kitchen. 'Wit's happened tae the fucking beans?' A ran doon fast as a could and told him a'd fed them tae the dugs.

'Those beans were fir yer supper. And now Wendy's deed. And we've got four dugs. D'ye understaund, pal?' Da started laughing but no in his usual way. In a way that a didnae understand wit he wis laughing aboot. He started throwing things aboot the kitchen and swearing and going mental.

'Da, a didnae know. A'm sorry.'

'If ye coulda jist won that bloody race. Is that no all ye could've done? That dug wis a waste of ma money. Am selling her back tae the shelter in the morning.'

A wisnae letting him sell ma dug. 'Yer no havin ma dug, Da.' A wis bawling so hard a wis on the floor and Da wis still going crazy. 'Nae wonder everyone calls you mad,' a said. 'You go bonkers over a tin of beans then try tae take ma dug away. Yer mad, jist like all the lads at school say.'

Da wis getting real mad at that. 'A telt ye no tae listen tae those boys.' He wis getting so mad but a couldnae stop what a said.

Ma belly jist ached so bad and ma whole body wis shaking. 'They say you went mad when Ma died. That you tried tae die too and left me tae die alongside you. Did you dae that Da? Did you leave me tae die as a baby?' He wisnae looking at me anymare. 'They say yer still trying tae kill me ye ken? Say yer starvin me tae death. They say yer a murderer Da, a really slow one. Killing me as slowly as you can.'

*

Da slept on the kitchen floor that night and a slept on the floor too, in ma bedroom, between the mattress and the dugs. A dinnae know wit a dreamed aboot that night but you were there and Da wis wi you and hugging you and saying he loved you. He wis saying he loved me too and ruffling ma hair. We were by the fish pond,

watching the trouts together and feeding them whatever we had
in oor pockets. We were feeding them loaf-ends and the bits in
the middle of the loaf, Swedish fish and fish supper too. A wis
jist a wee lad. A didnae ken much aboot things. But when a woke
up a knew exactly wit tae dae tae fix everything. A could keep ma
dug and stop Da fae being mad. He wouldnae go mad over things
like beans.

A came doon the stairs that morning, fair excited tae see Da's
reaction tae wit a'd done. He wis probably going tae gie me a hug
it wis that good. A wis fair proud of myself and you'll be proud of
me tae when you hear it. A heard some voices in the kitchen. It
wis the folk fae ootside old Wendy's the day afore and they were
bringing in crates of tins and jars and fruit with those god-damned
glassy cherries in them that a always spat oot. Nae scones or bacon
in sight. Da wis thanking them all and giving them all huge hugs.
But we didnae need their help cos a'd worked it all oot fir us.

'God, look at the size of you, wee man. Like a toothpick.' A big
man like the Hulk, but no so green, pulled me intae the kitchen,
all rough, by the oxters, pinching ma cheek like Wendy had done.
Hell, her family were all the same. 'Let's get some grub doon you,
eh, how's aboot that?'

Da looked at me funny like he knew wit a wis gonnae say.

A said, 'We dinnae need your help, cos a've sorted supper fir us,
Da,' and in ma hand, held up a plastic bag, brimming tae the top
wi three wee deed dugs.

Claire Deans
AN UNKINDNESS OF RAVENS

Jess left Glasgow with a bird lodged inside her abdomen, its wings thrashing.

She would not remember getting the lift down to the hospital car park and paying the parking fee which on any other day she would have considered scandalous. Perhaps she might have kicked up a fuss. Nor would she recall the Glasgow to Ardshiel coastal drive, where normally she might have stolen glances away from the bending road and out over the ocean. In one of the wee villages she would have bought sandwiches, carrot cake as a treat. She would have stopped at a viewing point to eat and admire the swell of the glittering waves as they caught the glint of the morning sun. She might have wound down the window to listen to the gulls squawking, the crashing of the waves. She would have revelled in the space, and the light, after months of being inside.

Instead, Jess found herself driving into Ardshiel as if she were somnambulant. **Ardshiel Toffee – Bank of Scotland – The Rumbling Tum – Black Bull Inn – Scottish Mill – Fish and Chips – Hyslop Hardware**

She parked at the Co-op, turned off the ignition and rolled down the window. For a few minutes, she sat with her eyes closed, inhaling long, slow breaths of air into her lungs, deep down to her abdomen, checking the status of the bird. With the motion and the classical music the bird must have been lulled.

The phone in her trouser pocket was vibrating against her hip.

She adjusted the rear-view mirror, checking her eyes for anything that might give her away. Tired, solemn eyes but no sign of tears. She tried on a smile. It looked fake and distorted and she let it fall. 'Oh Jess,' she whispered to her reflection. 'Poor Jess.' She sounded like her mum. She was thankful to put on the mask.

Rose, who had been standing blethering at the bakery section, came racing up the aisle when she saw her.

'Ruaridh is a grand worker indeed.' She was leaning in too close towards Jess. She smelt of cinnamon. 'Strength of a horse this morning, Jess. He's just finished restocking all those shelves.'

Rose nodded to an aisle where tins of soup and pulses were perfectly aligned on the shelves. It was as if Jess were viewing the scene for the first time. The metal gleamed too shiny, the lines were too straight, too perfect. She felt disorientated.

Rose was squinting at her as if sensing that something wasn't right. Please don't ask, thought Jess. Please don't ask. Although it was only a wee town and word would get out soon enough.

'How's the wisdom tooth?' It had been a topic of conversation for weeks.

Rose took the bait and began rabbiting on about her wisdom tooth, the pain she was enduring and the difficulty in getting a dentist appointment. For the first time, Jess noticed Rose's huge breasts. As she waved her arms around, her breasts were bouncing, the snapping buttons on her overall threatening to come apart, as if her breasts had had enough of being restrained. As if they wanted to riot.

Riotous melon breasts dashing up the condiment aisle.

This isn't funny, a stern voice in her head interjected. Then, suddenly, she was on the brink of tears. She looked away from Rose and down to her handbag, rubbing at it as if trying to remove a mark from the leather. Because God knows if she started greetin now she wouldn't be able to stop. And the last thing she wanted was a public scene in the grocer's on a Friday lunchtime with the eyes of the town upon her.

*

'Test me,' said Ruaridh.

'Mind that puddle.' Jess tugged at the sleeve of his rain jacket. 'Okay. How many planets are there in the solar system?'

'Eight.'

'Good lad. How many moons are there in our solar system?'

He paused. 'More than one hundred and fifty?'

'Well done. Who invented the telescope?'

'That's too hard.'

'Remember dad told you last night?'

'Someone with a funny name.'

'Galileo Galilei.' Jess smiled. 'I guess that does sound funny. How many moons does Pluto have?'

'Four moons.'

'Five moons. Almost right.' She high-fived him and laughed, forgetting the weight she was carrying.

'Dad said there's going to be a full moon tonight.'

'Is that right? Well, we'll need to make sure and have a wee look.'

At The Rumbling Tum, a new waitress scanned the room before leading them to a table in the corner.

'They'll be ending the distancing soon,' she said. 'Nicola made an announcement. The numbers are dropping.'

'About time we went back to normal,' said Jess.

She was feeling more confident, more in control now that she had Ruaridh by her side. She enquired after Erin, the regular waitress.

'Erin's returned to the island,' said the new waitress, 'her granny's sick with the virus.' While the new waitress wrote down their order, Jess's eyes were drawn to her small breasts.

'Will that be all, then?'

'Aye, thanks,' said Jess, looking up. Had she been caught? This was ridiculous.

The phone in her pocket began vibrating again. Cal would be worrying. *Phone me as soon as you get out*, he had instructed. She cradled her hand around the device until it stopped.

Jess watched Ruaridh carve thin slices from the ham and cheese before arranging them on top of the bread, topping it with chutney. He took a dainty bite.

Well, if this is the end at least you've taught him to eat with some manners, a voice in her head said. The bird in her abdomen stirred.

'Where's your food?' Ruaridh asked. Sometimes he surprised her with his observations. She told him that she was not hungry today because she had a bad stomach. Then she skimmed the foam and chocolate powder from the top of her cappuccino.

'You want this?' And she held the spoon out to allow him to skim it off with his lips. *You need to treat him like a man,* Cal had often said. Somehow she was in denial of the thick chestnut hair around his lips and chin. The broad-shouldered casing of a man, the mind of a child.

Jess lifted the lid from a ceramic jar shaped like a cupcake, and took out a sugar lump. She dropped it into her cappuccino and slowly stirred. As she replaced the lid on the jar, a thought popped into her mind. The ceramic cupcake was the shape and size of a small, pert breast. The shiny, glazed cherry on top could be a nipple. A tit.

She smirked as if someone had told her the punchline to a dirty joke. *This is no laughing matter,* a stern voice in her head spoke. It could be the doctor's voice.

. . . spare your nipple.

Jess let out a small sound like a creature weakened and in pain. Ruaridh was too busy tucking into his food to notice.

. . . spare your nipple.

The voice was so clear that the doctor might have been sitting opposite, transported from her office in Glasgow. The cold, white walls indifferent to distress.

. . . we can spare your nipple.

How generous, Jess had wanted to say. But that was when the bird had appeared and the power in its cruel wings had rendered her speechless.

'Have you bought the Paolo Nutini tickets yet?' Ruaridh's voice brought her back.

A birthday promise made for the future – six months down the line – if the pandemic allowed it, and if –

Now in her ribcage, the bird began to beat its wings. Is this how it is to be then? This continual terror? She glared into her cup, breathing deeply, willing the bird back down to the pit of her stomach, to settle it in a resting place, nesting.

And surely it must be a raven.

She was remembering a time when she had been taking Ruaridh to see the fishing boats return. As they cut through the park, Jess had seen a pair of ravens over at a nest toppled by the high wind. They were cracking the fallen eggs with their long, shiny beaks, croaking, tugging at the foetus inside. A sparrow was fluttering round in distress. They had attacked her too. Jess had lobbed one of her running shoes at the ravens but it had been too late.

'Nature can be cruel,' she had said, comforting Ruaridh.

Ruaridh was waiting for a reply. His blue eyes wide and unblinking.

'Not yet, son,' she said, 'but soon.'

When she was waiting at the till, she noticed a long knife lying next to a cake. Its blade was flashing as if speaking to her alone, transmitting her a message, reminding her of what was ahead.

The raven stirred.

'Have a good day,' said the new girl handing her the change.

'You too,' Jess said. But she was subdued now. This display of normality was draining.

They walked past the Ship Inn where men huddled together, their backs a wall against the bitter wind rising from the North Sea. Wisps of cigarette smoke drifted upwards.

'All right, Ruaridh lad?' one of them shouted.

'I'm grand, Mick,' shouted Ruaridh, delighted at being acknowledged.

Jess wanted to tell him not to give so much of himself because she remembered well the way they tormented him as youngsters. A feral pack of them scheming, kicking, punching, laughing, and she was sure that this savagery still lurked deep inside. But they weren't such big men now, their own suffering having cut them down to size. Mick McCarthy, Jess knew, had struggled with the drink after getting laid off at O'Brien's steelworks last year. Robbie Wallace lost Anna in the car crash and it was now only him and the bairn. Big Stu Patterson had buried his mum only last month. No one was laughing now.

Back at the car, Jess turned the ignition. The skies had opened up. Rain lashed at the windscreen, streaming down it, blurring her vision. Ruaridh inserted his Paulo Nutini disc into the CD player. The car was filled with music and the squeaking sound of the exhausted wipers. And now, driving towards home, all manner of thoughts flooded into her mind.

What if she refused treatment? Let it run rampant around her body. She would keep her hair then. Her *crowning glory*, as Cal called it. She would keep her dignity and escape the so-called treatment. Her mum had been all teeth and bones but still she kept smiling. Trying to be brave. Bald and emaciated down to her very essence. And it had all been for what? For nothing. For a few more months. She didn't *need* to tell Cal. It was her body. It was her choice. They could just carry on as normal. *Got the all-clear. Let's celebrate.* And she would open the bottle of Brut that had been chilling in the fridge since Christmas, since really there had been damn all to celebrate.

At the traffic lights, she glanced at Ruaridh gazing out the window, singing along tunelessly to songs he had learned over the years. He was somewhere far away from the dreich weather and the drama in her head. She felt an overwhelming rush of love. She could do this. She would get through this. She would do anything for the lad.

As she pulled into the driveway she could see Cal at the window – his face ashen under the afternoon's cold light. She wondered how long he had been standing there.

At the front door she could see close-up the strain of waiting. A tiny pulse throbbed up near his temple where his salt-and-pepper hair seemed to have become more salt than pepper.

'Hey,' he said, trying to meet her eyes. 'I've been phoning you. How did it go?'

'Not now,' she said, feeling suddenly angry at the unfairness of it. 'Not in front of the lad,' and she moved away to take off her mask.

'Test me, Dad,' said Ruaridh.

Once Ruaridh was settled in front of the TV, Cal came into the bedroom, sat on the edge of the bed and held her hand.

'Tell me,' he said.

Ducts and lobules An image of her breast had been displayed on the lightboard. *Lymph nodes* It was the focal point in the room, translucent and alluring in its half-moon curve. *Masses and microcalcifications* There was a nurse with a northern English accent who had called her *pet. It will take some time to process, pet.* But it had already been taken from her in the most terrifying language *histopathology report, invasive carcinoma, mastectomy, reconstruction* delivered in a matter-of-fact tone by the doctor with the wolfish eyebrows.

'My beautiful breasts,' she sobbed and for a few minutes she allowed herself the tears. Then she wiped them away. 'I'm sorry.'

'Permission to be human,' Cal responded. She forgave him the trite remark for what else could he say?

They sat next to Ruaridh on the sofa. He wanted to know how long she would be in hospital. She told him around one week. The placid expression on the lad's face didn't shift, but she could see a darkening in his blue eyes.

'Will you die?'

'No,' she said quickly. 'The doctors are going to make me well again. I'm not going to die.'

Because surely she will not die. She is still too young and fit to die.

Afterwards, she busied herself in the kitchen – turning on the oven, heating the lasagne, putting together a salad, as if everything was normal. But how could it be a normal day when she was imagining the songs they might play at her funeral? And later,

sitting around the TV she heard herself laughing too vigorously
at the sitcom.

'Try and eat something,' said Cal.

'Her stomach is bad,' said Ruaridh.

*

Years later, she remembers that she had wanted to soak in a lavender
bath, but after the dishes were cleared, Ruaridh had insisted that
they go out into the garden to see the full moon.

There had been an autumn chill in the air, but the earlier rain
had dried up leaving the sky clear and star-filled. From a distant
dimension she had heard Cal explaining asteroids and meteorites,
the lunar surface, massive cosmic impacts, craters. Ruaridh had
long lost interest and was spinning around the garden using his
arms as helicopter blades.

The moon had been sitting high above the horizon. She had
never seen it glow so brightly. Nor since that evening. It had given
itself to her like a gift. Fissures ran through it like the veins on her
breast. This scarred shimmering moon with its continual orbiting
was as enigmatic as her own body. And for the first time during
that long day, she had felt peace.

'Oh my god,' she had said. 'Look at it. Look at the moon.'

B. A. Didcock
THE BIRTHDAY PARTIES

Ma opens the shutters and lets it in. The Special Day. Bright and raw, just like the first time. This is good. A good sign. This means it will be super splendid, this Special Day.

But how slowly it rolls around! Da always gets a calendar from the man who supplies the feed, always nails it up over the telephone stand in the hallway. Ma tries not to watch the calendar for movement as she passes. Tries not to count off first the months and then the days until the time comes. Convinces herself this is the way to pull it in faster, like a doe turning her back on the fox. It never works. A week out she starts to fret and fidget. Picks at the skin on her fingers. The hum becomes a buzz, becomes a thing which shakes the plates off the walls.

But the Special Day is here now and Ma is thrilled. At the window she jigs on the spot, palms flat on the painted shutters.

Yes, yes, yes, yes!

Her excitement fogs the glass and a veil falls over the moor. She wipes at it. The hand comes back wet. The cold is a shock.

In the kitchen, high on a shelf, the precious family recipe book. She lifts it down carefully, remembering its weight. She taps the cover once, twice. Victoria Sponge this year or something fancier? What was it last year? What was it?

She peers into the dark pantry. Da might need to drive to town after he has dressed the twins. Violet will be in blue this year, Ivy in red. They take it turn and turn about. Pretty as a picture.

Five today! Her girls! Not properly until near midnight, but even so.

Angel cake, that was it. How could she forget?

*

For the fourth birthday, Da dresses up as a clown.

He ties Ma's old red plastic rain hat to his head with baler twine, smears butter on his face and pats it frost-white with flour. Clamps silver shillings tight in his eyes like a dead man and leaps around the kitchen, crashing into the furniture, trying to give Violet and Ivy the giggles. It's Ma who shrieks and howls when he trips on the carpet and lands in her lap.

Da always takes things too far.

Four candles are lit. Ma loves the way the flames dance in the twins' dark eyes. She sings . . .

Happy birthday to you!

. . . bellows it out . . .

Happy birthday to you!

. . . beckons Da to join in . . .

Happy birthday, our angels! Happy birthday to you!

Ma cuts the cake, four slices, but the girls leave theirs. Ma wonders if maybe it isn't sweet enough.

She gives Da the rest of it for the pigs.

*

The day before the twins' third birthday, Da takes Ma to the town. The sky is so low you could touch it if you jumped. The moor road is rutted from the rain. Ma presses her face to the window when they reach the Spot. *My love's bigger than a Cadillac.* If Da hears, he says nothing.

Ma hates leaving home, can't bear to be apart from her girls even for an hour. But they have magazines in the shops in town and she needs inspiration. When Da strides off to meet the seed man and visit the council office about the latest nosy letter, she chooses the busiest shop she can see and enters. Noiseless, nervous.

One magazine has pictures of cakes. Exactly what she needs. The girls will love them. She takes her nail scissors to it when the shopkeeper is busy with a customer, folds the pages carefully, places them in her handbag and puts back the torn and tattered magazine.

A woman sees her and shakes her head. Ma turns, hisses. The woman hurries away.

Now Ma is angry. Ashamed. Scared. Glancing up, the holes in the paper have become dead eyes. She straight away tries to shoo the thought but cannot. Memories settle round her like the debris that once covered the Spot.

She goes to find Da but still the curtain won't drop.

*

The snow falls all day when the girls turn two. The moor is a dirty, crumpled sheet, low light making shadows of its creases. A scene too ugly and harsh for the Special Day: Ma yearns to make it pretty, tuck it up, fold it neat.

Instead she opens all the windows so she can sing. The noise brings in Da from the workshop. He's covered in fat and blood but Violet and Ivy must be used to the sight by now. They don't scream or cry, just sit patiently. Such good girls.

Later they drink milk still warm from the goat. It's a beautiful birthday despite the snow.

It's a week later when the first of the nosy letters arrives.

*

To mark the twins turning one, Ma tells Da she wants them to have a gift. They throw it back and forth and think they've settled on a rocking horse until Ma has a better idea. A real pet!

Within a week Da has killed the owl with poison. He still has the wire, hemp wool and borax, and all the tools and sharps for the skinning and preserving, for the draining of the lipids.

May as well put it to use, lass.

Da hates things going to waste.

He settles down to it at the kitchen table after tea one night. He likes to sing as he works, a rowdy song he learned in the army. Ma hates it but she lets him.

Da mounts the owl on a panel of yew, but Ma makes him tether it with a jess just in case.

Don't want it flying off, Da, do we? Imagine how upset the girls would be if it escaped?

*

A year to the day earlier.

It's near midnight when the woman wakes and feels the earth seem to shiver. She hurries to the window. All wrong. Light where none should be – an orange glare a mile away to the west.

From the bedroom she can see wreckage scattered across the moor. Metal, great knuckles of it, in graceless twists and blunted spirals. Glowing like old bone.

Her husband dresses hurriedly and leaves in the four-wheel. He soon returns. She hears the bite of the tyres on the track, sees his arm through the window beckoning her.

In the trailer, lass.

She pulls back the tarp and sees them for the first time – her girls. Her angels. So peaceful in sleep, though one has her head bent at a crazy angle. She'll decide afterwards this is Ivy.

She helps him carry them inside. The blood-hiss in her ears makes her think she might burst with pleasure but she is calm, careful, tender.

Found them by the Stones.

This will become the Spot.

Will you be gentle with them, lass?

Yes. She will cherish them, place them above all other things in life. They will need time and special care, but she trusts him. He has the tools and the knowledge.

They were still buckled into their seats.

Then they are gone to the barn to begin their new life, and there is only the restless barking of the dogs and her own internal humming. She is dizzy with the suddenness. It is like a death in reverse. For years, only her and him. For years, almost completely alone in the house on the high moor. Now, a birth. Twins! A Special Day has come, out of the dark winter night, and she will forever give thanks.

Long before dawn she turns on the wireless and already there is news of it. Somewhere over their heads as they slept, an explosion or a fault. But she doesn't want to hear it, stabs desperately at the buttons. She finds a song instead. 'Not Fade Away' by Buddy Holly & The Crickets.

I'm gonna tell you how it's gonna be . . .

Much better. She jigs a little on the spot.

. . . You're gonna give your love to me . . .

Her face at the window turns up but she sees only stars.

Samantha Dooey-Miles
NICE THINGS

There's a split second for us to decide whether we're going to address the issue or pretend it doesn't exist. She doesn't look the type who'll be comfortable about the situation, embarrassment's probably brewing in her, so I go, 'Great jacket.'

Her hands flit up and touch the lapel of her black biker jacket, her face relaxes. 'Thanks, same to you.' There, now we can move past the mild awkwardness of us both wearing the same thing. Except, and I'm not being rude, these are the facts, hers is clearly vegan leather and not the best quality. It has a rubbery sheen of cheapness, I bet it squeaks when she moves. Mine on the other hand cost £350, plus the interest I'll accrue paying it off slowly from my credit card. The fresh leathery tang it gives the air around me makes me feel cool, like a small debt is worthwhile.

We're both in this pub function room, near Central Station, for Heather's boring boyfriend Donald's birthday. Heather's my childhood best friend and Shirley works with her doing whatever it is urban planners do. While this is the first time we've ever met, I do know a lot about her. She leaves love heart emojis under any selfie Heather posts on Instagram, she found her ex-husband having sex with another man on their honeymoon, she thought she had cancer last summer but the lump was benign. I stare down with unease at the swirly patterned carpet, the kind you only ever see in pubs, realising Heather must have shared the more salacious parts of my life with Shirley, too. My boob job and the brief period where I slept with a lot of strangers to get over my ex-girlfriend. We both dump our stuff onto a heaped chair in the corner of the party, which appears as lacklustre as Donald's personality. Shirley says she's going to the bar, I follow, this feels like a night where alcohol will be necessary.

'Heather was mentioning how busy work is for her. Is it the same for you?'

'Yeah, it's all a bit crazy with the High Street redevelopment project.'

'Right.' I draw out the word as I watch a barman approach. Twirling my debit card in my hands to demonstrate I have the funds ready and waiting. He chooses to serve some old boy, which is the right thing to do as he was here well before me. Still – it's annoying.

While we wait, Shirley isn't offering much in the way of quality chitchat. She manages a 'It's a good turnout, isn't it?' before I decide to test the waters on a subject I never get to talk to anyone about but she may be the prime audience for – how awful I find the birthday boy and how strange it is to me wonderful Heather believes this loser is the one.

'Do you know Donald well?'

Just as she starts talking, I remember everything she's about to say. Heather has told me it all before. 'We've known each other since we were kids. He's my brother's friend from school and one of my ex-husband's best friends from playing rugby together. One day me and Heather were walking down Bath Street and bumped into him and that was that.' A glaze comes over Shirley's eyes as if this is the most romantic tale imaginable.

I'm pleased I didn't begin stronger with 'So Donald's a dull bastard, isn't he?' I struggle to know how to follow up, 'So their relationship . . .'

'. . . seems perfect, doesn't it?' Which, thank God, is the exact moment the barman gets round to serving me. I order Shirley the vodka and coke she asks for and the largest available size glass of sauvignon blanc for me. When I hand Shirley her drink, it marks the end of our interaction, a farewell gift. I can't have done a very good job of imparting this information as she follows me back to where we dumped our things and keeps me locked in conversation. For at least twenty minutes she describes to me each room in her one-bedroom flat in Shawlands and how she has redecorated it as a 'true of expression of herself' having 'compromised far too much' for her ex. I'm not a total arsehole so I do pretend to be interested. Actually, I am interested enough to ask to see pictures of the bathroom after she describes the decor as 'highly romantic'. What this means, I find out, is she's decoupaged the walls with images of cherubs and Roman gods like Laurence Llewelyn-Bowen used to do on *Changing Rooms*.

'You have a real eye for design,' I say, passing her phone back. The wine has kicked in so I'm feeling warm and fuzzy towards everyone. Which would make this the optimum moment to head over to Donald and wish him a happy birthday. This is my best chance of coming across as genuinely meaning it but he's deep in conversation with a really short guy and I can't be arsed interrupting. Shirley is swiping on her screen to show me her bedroom. 'For this room I wanted to make it an ultra-feminine boudoir. When Tony was about, he always insisted every room had a touch of masculinity.'

The slideshow of silky floral bedsheets ends when Heather joins us. 'Shirl did you see your brother's here?' Heather points in the general direction of a chubby, balding man in a checked shirt who looks like sixty per cent of the other men in this place. Shirley vacates. Once she's out of earshot, Heather asks, 'How'd you like her flat?'

'It's surprisingly characterful for someone so dull.'

Heather loudly sucks the last of her vodka through two tiny black straws, the kind I thought no longer existed due to all the sea life they killed. 'You think everyone is boring.'

'Most people are. Consider yourself lucky I find you fascinating.'

Whatever witty retort Heather is about to respond with is never said as there's a shriek from behind us and then the crash of a glass smashing. From a far-off corner two men cheer upon hearing the breakage. Shirley shouts, 'What the hell is he doing here?'

Looking over my shoulder Heather groans, 'Shit, the ex-husband's here,' and dashes off. I finish the dregs of my drink watching the drama unfold. The ex-husband is another chubby man in a checked shirt. He's talking to Shirley's brother who's the diplomatic piggy in the middle. Saying a few words to the ex in as politically neutral a voice as possible, before turning and relaying the message to Shirley. I can only make out snippets of it, 'he's my friend as well,' 'we agreed I got social events in March,' and finally, 'you should have thought about *that* in Mexico.' I'm so engrossed, it takes me a minute to notice Heather is giving Donald an earful. It's not often you get to witness a row in public, two at the same time is quite a sight. The first bout ends with Shirley shouting, 'You're welcome to stay, it's boring as shit – which'll suit you down to the ground.' I find this extremely offensive. She doesn't even have the manners to say goodbye, she barges past me, grabs her coat, and leaves.

When Heather is done with Donald she comes over, her brow sweaty from arguing, 'Fancy getting out of here?'

'Are you sure?' I'm already reaching for my stuff.

'Yeah, just Donald thinking about Donald and no one else as per bloody usual.'

My delight at Heather realising Donald is flawed is extinguished when I pick up what should be my gorgeous new jacket, only to discover it's Shirley's cheap imitation.

I rummage through the pile, displacing the coats and bags that were there long before I arrived. An effort I know is futile but I continue until Donald sneaks up, 'You're not leaving are you Heather? Come on, it's my birthday.' I grab Shirley's jacket and walk with Heather towards the door, 'Happy birthday!' I shout, not sounding like I mean it at all.

*

The exchange of stolen goods is supposed to happen on Tuesday when I meet Heather for drinks. I have the offending item in a canvas bag at my feet, ready to hand over. I've even made sure to fold it as best I can so the plastic leather doesn't get indented. Despite the lack of jacket being an all-consuming thought since

Saturday night, I'm careful to ask Heather how she's doing before I ask for it back.

Heather replies, 'I'm great. The first phase of the project launched so things are easing up at work.' There's no need to investigate on the Donald front because she's already texted me to let me know they made up. Still, Heather feels the need to prove the all-rightness of their relationship by telling me 'Bit sore.' She takes a sip from a glass that appears to be filled with cranberry juice. 'When we fall out, Donald likes to make up hard.' If she's permitted to invoke the image of Donald going at it, I'm sure as hell okay to say, 'Got my coat?' I put the bag on the table in expectation of the swap taking place. It doesn't. Heather clears the table, 'Yeah, about that. Shirley was off sick yesterday. Was in today and had totally forgotten about it. I'll drop it round yours on Friday?'

I try to express understanding with a tight-lipped smile while wondering if I can ask Shirley for dry cleaning money to eradicate her sick germs from the leather.

*

The wait until Friday about kills me. On Thursday night I type out a Facebook message to Shirley:

Hey!
Was so great finally meeting you the other night!
Please can you remember to give Heather my jacket tomorrow?
I've got a date on Saturday and it's vital for the outfit I have planned.
I'd REALLY appreciate it.
Thanks!

I read it back, remove an apostrophe, add it back in, take out the mention of when I saw her and then delete the whole thing. I sound pathetic, even though it's my property. There's an innate tragic quality to requesting the return of a belonging when that person knows they should've already given you it back.

Come Friday I regret not pressing send when Heather turns up to mine with wine and nothing else because 'To be honest, Shirley's being funny about it.'

On Saturday my date, Roderick, tells me I look lovely. I'm wearing a midi floral dress with a black denim jacket and I look fine but niggling is the knowledge I could have looked fantastic if not for sodding Shirley and boring Donald and his idiot friends. Waiting for the bill for our extremely average Italian to come, I tell Roderick (he insists on the whole name, never ever Roddy, despite it being infinitely nicer) the saga of Shirley. His complete indifference to the story and his unsubtle mention that I can get dinner 'next time' – when I thought it was obvious neither of us were enjoying ourselves enough to bother to do this again – means I decide I won't sleep with him. Before I get on the subway, I do let him kiss me with tongues and briefly cup my left breast to be sure he does nothing for me. After a few minutes, I'm sure.

*

My breaking point comes the following week. Heather is dodging my messages, I'm avoiding Roderick's voicemails, and a scroll on Facebook reveals Shirley is all right enough to post an image of a grey sky, with a rambling caption about sadness and waiting for rainbows to appear. My thumbs hover over the keyboard tempted to comment **At the end of the rainbow will I find my jacket?** Then I get an email alert letting me know my credit card statement is in, including the hundreds of pounds I owe for the one fancy thing I own but the universe has decided I can't actually possess. I fling my phone across the room, onto the other sofa. I can't afford to buy a new one while I'm drowning in jacket debt.

Among the cushions it starts to dully ring. It's Heather. I accept her call kneeling on the carpet feeling utterly miserable, the way I do the day before my period comes. I wonder if I've had my fill of bad times and Heather is about to offer hope. She doesn't.

'You're not getting your jacket back.' Heather delivers this information as if it's more irritating for her to have to tell me, than it is for me to receive.

'Why not?'

Heather exhales like I'm annoying her for asking for follow up. 'Because the police have it.'

'What did she do?' I screech.

'She didn't do anything. She was sexually assaulted on the way home the night she took it.'

Oh.

*

Six months later, it's freezing, heavy coat weather when the police release my jacket, the case closed due to lack of evidence. With no forensic material of use to be found on it, it's free. Unlike Shirley's dress and shoes which remain sealed away somewhere in case more leads come to light. Which they won't, brown-haired sex cases approximately five foot ten are everywhere. The detective who gave me a form to sign to confirm I'm collecting my belongings fits the description, so does the man who drives the bus that drops me off at the dry cleaners.

Whether I'll be able to bring myself to wear it again I don't know but whatever happens, it needs to be cleaned. 'Twice,' I tell the man at the counter who cocks an eyebrow as if this doesn't make sense. I give him the huge paper evidence sack, it crunches and rustles louder than my voice as he takes it from me, 'Are you able to clean it twice?' I repeat.

'There's no need. Once will be enough to get it in good order. It looks like it's hardly been worn.' He's examining the garment as he speaks, running his fingers along the zip and the stitching looking for imperfections he has to document on the little tab of cardboard they give you in exchange for your item.

'No, it has to be twice. It has,' I can think of no better way of describing it, 'bad energy.'

His face sets like he's figured out he's dealing with a simpleton and will have to tell me 'no' again in a way I'll be able to understand. I can't face a back and forth so I tell a fib because I know it'll get us to the end quicker, 'I was assaulted in it. I need any trace of it gone.' And while the police didn't find any DNA on it, there are remnants of lots of things about that night still clinging to the leather.

His cheeks flush, he finishes filling in the ticket, the only sound the scratch of his pen on the paper. It's not until I'm outside I notice he only charged me for one clean.

*

The rejuvenated jacket sits on a hook next to the door through a long Scottish winter that only shifts in May. At first I keep it separate from everything else; it turns out no number of cleans can fully remove the taint for me. Until suddenly the whiff of horror around it recedes. The sun shines for more hours of the day, making the world seem less bleak until I go out and realise it's not yet as warm as it looks. It's light jacket weather. Which leads to me putting the jacket on one day to pop to the corner shop for milk. I wear it another time to go post a letter, on another to put the bins out. The cumulative effect of these short jaunts is the incident begins to feel distant. It disappears completely when, one Friday night, I decide to wear it to meet Heather for dinner.

Wearing it is everything I dreamed of when I purchased it. Waiting outside the restaurant I feel so confident I'm not even compelled to fanny about on my phone to avoid people seeing me alone. When Heather arrives she greets me with, 'You look great. Love the jacket, is it new?'

'Scrubs up all right, doesn't it?'

The smile falls from Heather's face, 'You mean it's *the* jacket?' Her brow wrinkles, 'I don't know how you can wear it.'

I ream off all of the ways I've justified my continued wear of the piece despite its history, 'I wasn't there. It didn't happen to me. To me it's a jacket I lost and found again that cost me £350. I can't afford to throw away £350. For me, it's a nice thing I bought. Aren't I allowed nice things?'

Heather opens the door to the restaurant, 'I think the nice thing is a man didn't try and rape you.'

I don't say this out loud, but I think the nice thing is really the jacket.

John Duffy
AVERAGE CONTENTS, 48

A gift for fidgets, a matchbox, rattling
in your pocket as you walked. You'd lift it,
hold its neat squat shape, smooth except
where sandpaper cat's tongue licked
your fingertips. Middle finger and thumb
slid the drawer and slid it back again,
pushing against the other's push.
You'd shake it to test how full it sounded.
The piny smell of fresh stacked matchsticks.
The jostling throng of pale red busbies,
primed for their moment of glory.
Into your hands, cupped against draughts,
you scraped a bowl of light and a brief blue
smoky veil. Then one quick wrist flick
to dowse the glim. Pocket the box again.

Thomas Elson
WHAT WE TALK ABOUT WHEN WE DON'T TALK

We've been together most of your life. And, I have only one rule.

An eighty-four-year-old widow, hands trembling and crying on her marital bed – remembering her ninth year on earth and the death of her mother in 1919. Too afraid and confused to say, *They took turns flicking holy water on my mother's casket before it was lowered. First dad, then Josephine, then Eddie, then – when it came to me I couldn't. I threw it on the ground and ran home.* Her face wet, she sat in silence. The girl who walked home each day after school with the sixteen-year-old boy, suddenly and silently absent from her seventh-grade class.

Sitting by themselves in front of their Sylvania halo-of-light console television screen. Lights down and volume up as minds veered from her husband's burned sister dying in a foreign state to her three children soon to be motherless. The single available channel tuned to Ed Sullivan's *Toast of the Town*.

A German war bride, during the annual church supper at the municipal building, her palm held across her stomach, unable to empty her mind. She remembers. *That poor girl in the basement house next to us. Her father renting her out to men for fifty dollars a month. No wonder she did what she did to him.* Then turned away.

Daniel's best friend, the ten-year-old no one talked about, dead within days. His mother's friend standing in their kitchen on the evening of the funeral, stared out the screen door, her arms clenched across her chest, thought but never said, *His family was haunted by that image of their ten-year-old – waxen and pasty-faced. With the rest of his body covered. Just a few days before they were water-skiing.*

A young woman, eyes fixed on the hospital floor tiles, shivers in silence near the window of a group therapy room, body shaking, her thoughts on childhood, her voice silent after she struggled to approach a nurse – sheltered behind the nurses' station. The young woman shuddered – remained silent. *Before I started school. If my father's friends were over, he'd dress me up like a go-go dancer.* Her breathing hitched. *He would stand me on the table, and say, Dance for me, darlin. Then pat me, and hand me to his friend.*

An old man cries in a crowded room six blocks from his childhood home. When he was a boy, his father would prance wildly in front of him and cross his eyes – imitating his son's strabismus.

A grown man, his face in tears, arms scarred by burns received when, as a three-year-old, he urinated on his father's boots. His father spread lighter fluid around the boot, dumped the three-year-old in the centre, and tossed a lighted match into the circle.

A thirty-nine-year-old man, in a dead-end treatment centre in a small town in the western part of the state – in recovery for cocaine addiction – decided not to risk telling his counsellor about pressing a pillow into his lover's face and shoving it down for long minutes – after months of attending to his dying partner who lay splotched, festering, and boiling from a disease not yet named.

A middle-aged woman isolating in a corner of a hospital room, after learning her father was killed for reasons yet silent. For decades quiet about a phone call from her father's paramour, answered by her – then five years old. The child's contralto voice mistaken for her mother's. That call followed by a divorce; her father's imprisonment, their visits through a twelve-by-twelve glass window, then silence. She watches nurses remove the needles from her father's veins as the room is prepped for the next person.

You know who I am.

We've been together most of your life.

And, you know my one rule.

Ophira Gottlieb
THE HUNDUN

High on heather-bruised mountains
torchless wanderers die of the dark
trip, fell, goat, crag,
clambering,
nothing but a set of eyes for stars

nothing but the deep-set eyes of sheep
constellating,
indicating compass points like compasses do
and you, now satiated, walk into the bog:

we have just made love like lovers do.
You had turned me over so that I could watch the moon
but instead I met the glistening eyes of sheep
gristling with meat or fat
with heaving milk. White as the sheen

on the surface of the water –
cloudy evening residue. We are uncertain.
Hesitant as herons we enter
making light of the things our feet find in the water

like rotting wool, like pointed skull
walk on
we are wanderers too, if you think about it,
torchless, dying of the dark
but I don't, no, I don't think at all.

Hamish Gray
POSSIL MARSH

The muttering of oaths and expletives finished with two loud clonks and a drawn-out groan.

'Aw thank Christ for concrete.'

Aidan collapsed next to the bench, weary after having dragged it through flowerbeds and past huffing joggers for the better part of half an hour. He massaged his hands and craned his neck round to the park behind him; a football tumbled between two piles of jumpers. As the cheer faded, Aidan drew a finger through one of the twin trenches the bench legs had gouged into the grass, then scrubbed the mud off against his jacket.

He mumbled, 'Thank Christ he just does weekends,' before chuckling as he scratched his beard. The wind picked up, sending an empty packet of crisps tumbling over Aidan's legs. He rubbed the moisture from his fingers onto his jeans. 'What a fog,' he said, a pensioner glancing at him as she shuffled by.

'I was saying the weather's a bit shit,' he called after her.

Aidan watched the old woman go, before turning to the bench. He patted its arm. 'Right Cherlie,' he said. 'We're moving. Don't worry, we're moving.' Aidan clambered to his feet, put his hands on his hips and pushed forward until his back cracked, then with a snort he bent down and gripped the bench. Tensing his legs, he lifted the end up and began to drag it towards the traffic lights. He dotted the pavement as he walked, the bench legs scraping a line through each muddy footprint. A cyclist waiting at the crossing tightened his lips as Aidan approached.

'Mind getting the lights?' Aidan asked him.

The stopped cars drove off as the light changed green, and the cyclist pedalled after them.

'Cheers,' Aidan muttered. The bench began to topple to the side as he removed one hand to push the button, before jerking it back to sort his grip, too late to stop the bench falling to the ground. Aidan stepped back and flexed his fingers.

'You dinnae make it easy, Cherlie,' he said to the bench, grinning.

'Tilly. Heel,' a man's voice commanded. On the opposite pavement, a mother pulled her pouting child closer as a terrier sniffed at their shopping bags. The dog looked back at its owner, tail wagging as it jumped towards him. The green man sounded; Aidan blinked. He stooped for the bench and backpedalled across the road. A Renault honked him on as he reached the other side, hauling the bench over the kerb. He lowered it to the ground, then backed away to survey the mass of branches and birds' nests that marked the perimeter of Possil Marsh. He clicked his tongue and approached the undergrowth, squinting through the brambles. He grabbed a handful of branches and pulled them back; a magpie cawed at the intrusion and flapped off.

'All good there, pal?' a voice called from behind him.

'Aye. Fine,' Aidan replied, without looking back.

'Aw is that you Aidan?'

He twitched his head round a fraction, then backed out of the scrub.

'All right Sammy? Never knew it was you,' he said, his breath stilted. 'Thought you were just weekends?'

'It's Sunday, Aidan,' the park ranger said.

'Ah right enough.' Aidan nodded, looking at the space he'd cleared. 'Here, you got a second?' He clumped more of the branches together and twisted them towards the ground. 'Hold these down.'

'Is that from Maryhill?' Sammy asked.

'What?' Aidan glanced back. The park ranger was staring at the bench, his brow furrowed. 'Oh aye, it was by the duckpond.' He returned to the undergrowth.

'Right.' Sammy's frown deepened. 'What's it doing here?'

The rummaging stopped. 'It's for Cherlie, man,' Aidan explained. 'He was keen on Possil.'

Sammy nodded slowly. He slipped his phone back into his pocket.

'Anyway.' Aidan stood and dusted his hands against his jacket. 'I'll be away through soon.'

Sammy shook his head. 'I'll get the van; drive you round the entrance.'

'Aye?' Aidan raised his eyebrows. He scratched his beard. 'You sure? I can get through myself.'

'I'm sure, Aidan. I'll only be a minute. Meet you back here, you understand?'

'Aye. Yeah no, aye. I understand. I'll wait here.'

'Right. See you in a bit.'

'Right enough.'

Sammy crossed at the lights and walked past a row of tenement housing; Aidan inspected the buildings. He knew there'd be eyes watching him – curtain twitchers, his grandad used to call them. The gardens were empty, save for a pair of trousers which hung alone on a washing line, kicking at the wind. The right leg jerked to the side as the left spasmed backwards. Aidan stared at them, condensation humming from his mouth, his hand rising to rub the bristles of his neck. The fog had lifted somewhat; the sun even managed to poke a hole through the clouds. A white van came to a stop a little way down the road. Sammy climbed out and clicked open the side door. He beckoned forward. Nodding back, Aidan hoisted the bench up and sidled over to Sammy, who backed into the van to help bring it in.

'We'd better go slow,' he said.

Aidan agreed as he clambered into the passenger seat, sweeping bits of dried leaves and twigs from its surface. Sammy got in next, checking the mirrors before pulling out onto the road. A half-empty cup sat by the gearstick, surrounded by loose coins and chewing gum packets. Aidan shuffled around and stared out the window as they drove.

'How've you been?' Sammy asked.

Aidan watched as a man opened a garden gate. His terrier charged through and leapt to nip at the pair of twitching trousers. 'No much,' he mumbled.

'What?'

'No much I said.'

'Aw sorry, I asked how you were.'

'Oh aye. Right. Doin' awa'.'

The van slowed to a stop by some traffic lights. Sammy tapped at the wheel.

'Saw your pals by the canal,' he said.

Aidan grunted.

'Craig an' that. Seemed all right.'

Nothing.

'You seen them recently?'

Aidan wrinkled his brow. 'Maybe if they werenae down the canal getting pished I would have.' He jerked his head to Sammy. 'What do you think? Could have helped me with aw this, eh?'

'Aye,' the park ranger spoke quietly, changing gears as the lights turned green. 'Right enough.'

Aidan fidgeted in his seat. He started to chew on the skin next to his fingernail. Sammy spun the wheel round as they turned a corner to Possil Marsh's visitor centre, lurching to a stop behind the café. He put the handbrake on and pulled out the keys, then started tapping them against the wheel. Eventually he asked, 'Did you talk to him, before it happened?'

Aidan stopped chewing. 'Aye, I told him. Cherlie, I said, go home and have a wank. Have a wank an' that'll get it out your system.'

A family of pink anoraks wandered past the van.

'He'd been planning it, I think. I keep telling the guys that but none of them say anything.' Aidan stared at the dashboard, thinking back to the trousers on the washing line.

Sammy unclipped himself and stepped out. 'Dinnae put it near the path,' he said. 'An' avoid the reeds, snipes nest in them.'

Aidan nodded. He didn't look at Sammy.

'Take care pal.'

'Aye, you too.'

The two men parted ways.

Aidan stumbled through Possil Marsh, humming tunelessly. The fog was fading quick. The farther he travelled, the more the marsh opened up to him. Ignoring the path, he cut straight through the mud to the heart of the wildlife reserve. Aidan cursed as his foot sunk into the fen. He shoogled his leg to wrest it free, but gave up, and took a second to breathe and rub his creased brow. Some bird, Cherlie would have known what kind, swooped overhead, its wings outstretched. As he watched it glide towards a patch of birch trees, he thought of a spot to leave the bench. With a *shlunk*, he dislodged himself and backed off onto surer footing.

Aidan marched through the grasslands. The distant loch inched closer, set ablaze by the retreating sun. The ground held him back some, leeching at his shoes as he stumbled through another patch of reeds whose umber heads bobbed at the stranger, their thin bodies rattling in the wind. Aidan paused to do up his jacket.

'Mind this, Cherlie?' he spoke quietly, thumbing with the zipper. 'Shit,' he said, catching his finger.

A frog sprung from the reeds and danced across the sea of rushes. Bits of tangled flora shivered with each spring forward. Aidan shuffled back to the bench and resumed the journey. Before long he could hear the faint muttering of a stream. Aidan strained to listen, glad to be guided through the endless brown of the marsh. The wind grew stronger as he stamped onwards, whistling as it weaved between the reeds. In turn, the reed-heads shook; by the dimming light they had turned to ochre rattles, and were now dense enough to be as walls. Aidan approached a clearing. The mutter of the stream had risen to a gurgle by the time he set the bench down. He remembered this place. Remembered the time they'd stood here as a group and blethered on about things that didn't matter now and weren't all that important then, could still see a crumpled can in the rushes, caked with mud, a pool of dirty water in its mouth. What he liked most about that night was the singing. A few football chants from the ones who wanted to hear them, but mostly good, old songs. Ones they'd been taught in school. Cherlie's voice had been the nicest, which surprised Aidan, and he'd said as much to him.

'When the fuck do we ever sing, man?' Cherlie had laughed. 'When do we ever sing?'

Wind whistled. The stream gurgled through ochre rattles. Aidan thought of Cherlie's singing as the moon crept up behind him. The bench stood where he'd set it down, with its back to the reeds and the legs already sinking into the mud. Maybe it was the murk, but the wood started to look soft, and warm.

'Cherlie,' he said. 'I've been having problems with my door. The key keeps getting stuck in the lock; if it goes, I'm scunnert, and I'm thinking if that happens I'll need to stay with Malcolm for a few days. I cannae wait till the last Friday of the month, and they'll no be bothering with giving me an advance. They'll no— Just trust me, they'll no bother.' He swallowed. 'Malcolm has this reeking dish towel in his kitchen, the thing's as old as I am. I can never think why he keeps it; I think he must ken how it stinks, there's no a spot of white left on it. I can't think . . . Craig has his bairn, I wouldnae be comfortable going to his for any length of time, even if it's just for a few nights.' He thumbed the zip of his jacket. The reeds had stopped shaking. Aidan glanced away from the bench. 'Your mum told me about her sleeping tablets, I'm thinking I'll have to ask for the brand.' He shook his head and cast his eyes up at the night sky. 'I'm thinking you made a mistake with that, Cherlie. She's so fucking miserable now, I—' His voice gave way to a rattling breath.

The bench sat silent. Aidan wondered if they were talking about him, down by the canal. They'd have cans and a fire, maybe Malcolm brought his radio. He thought about telling them where he'd been, but he wasn't sure what the point would be. Clearing his throat, he slumped forward, then – hand on the bench to steady himself – he moved away from the spot, and began to march across the marsh, made small by the sight of the moon.

Julie Laing
A MISCHIEF

People are starting to notice the rats. We've always known they're there, two for every one of us, six feet away, but up till now they've mostly kept themselves to themselves. Not so much these days though. A month or so ago when I was heading to work, one strolls across the road ahead of me, silhouetted in sunrise like some kind of hero. If it wasn't for the baldy tail it could have been a cat. Unusual. To be fair, the *Daily* _____ did warn us that rodents as big as rabbits could be invading homes this winter.

When I tell you about it you shudder, *For fuck's sake*, and go all PTSD over that rat flit you saw when you were wee. Scores of them, flowing away from the old granary towards the shipyard, and you and your pals running up the embankment to get out their way. I wonder where they ended up, and you open up your arms to the room: *Where do you think? They were hungry.* The thought of them nesting in our cavities and foraging at night makes me shiver too. I google rats and a few links in they become kind of human. I tell you they laugh if they're tickled – too high for us to hear right enough – and when they're happy their ears turn pink.

Weil's disease, you say, and you're not having it when I tell you that these days human infection in the UK is minimal. You remember jaggy paws over your feet and still piss in a bottle rather than cross the hall at night.

*

The next one's a couple of days later and you're actually with me. We're in the drive-thru queue and you spot it while I'm reading the menu. It's that same shudder of yours that makes me turn to look. There it is, donnering along the top of the wall where the bins are, totally unfazed by all the cars and kids. It looks like it knows there's absolutely fuck all we can do. You shake your head.

You don't even have to be dirty to see them now. I suggest we mention it on the feedback, but you think it's pointless and don't even order when it's our turn – even though it was the last day for that limited edition veggie burger.

So, when Em turns up last week with the kids and everything in bags, you're not having it at all, until she tells us what's happened. I can't get it out of my head.

It just jumped out of the fireplace into the living room. She has to keep saying it to believe it herself. They're sitting there, watching Strictly, and there's this scratching, but she just thinks it's a bit of DIY next door and turns up the volume. Can you imagine? You're just hanging out in your jammies on a Friday night and a fucking rat leaps into your living room. The kids screaming, it screaming, and the worse thing is they've no idea where it went. So, I tell you she's coming in with me, the kids can have The Wee Man's room till he's back and you can have the couch so you've still got the telly. The Council will put traps and poison down and they'll be home soon as. Em's a bit steaming with the stress, angry, and saying *If their bloody pals hadn't been on strike for so long they wouldn't have so many fucking vermin to hunt down.* You pipe up from the couch, *So it's their fault then, is it?*

I try to back you up and remind her it was manky before. People have too much stuff for the bins and I've seen seagulls topple more than one lid. You look round from the couch like I'm talking shite. *So it's our fault now?* I can't work out the right answer, so shut up.

Em's reading her phone and tells us that, actually, we have the most rats per head of any UK city. You're like, *Is that right, Mrs Google? I wonder why that is then.* I roll my eyes behind your back. You're still grumbling with your face back in your laptop. *Same everywhere, so it is.*

She's looking out the window at the back court. *How about a wee bit of collective action at the midden while we're waiting for poverty to end?* You shuffle your neck on your shoulders and look up.

You don't touch that. Do you hear me? That's the Council's mess and it stays till they sort it. Things only change when they've broken down.

That'll be any day now then, she says, and I go into la-la-la mode and joke that at least the seagulls are good for something these days, eating the babies. Baby rats. Not actual babies. *Yet,* you say. Em pipes up again.

Anyway, if that's the reason, how come us 'poor folk' manage to chuck so much food? Jay and Elle look round, nervy, like they shouldn't be eating their crisps. You're leaning across the table, looking her up and down as if to say you could be doing with throwing away a bit more grub, but catch onto yourself when I jerk my head towards the kids. You retreat to the 1970s where there was no fast food, folk knew what side they were on . . . But I'm lost. Is it our fault or not? You'll say anything to win so I give up, but Em's locked on: *Who was in charge then? Labour?*

Oh, oh. I shrug between youse as if to say, it makes no difference. You're shouting, *Of course it matters who's in charge, for fuck's sake. This lot don't give a shit what happens to us.* Wee Jay starts sobbing again.

Which lot's that then? asks his mum. *The Tories or the Nats?*

I'm done. She should pack it in. I rustle up the kids and head out to get the tea in, leaving you pair to dish out the blame to opposing elites . . . You'd think she'd mind her gob while she's sleeping under your roof.

Anyway, when we get back, Em's feeding the baby and you've put the plates and everything out. Truce. Elle and Jay see it in your faces and get giggly. The chippie lifts spirits and we hang out for a bit as if everything's all right.

Actually, the more you find out about them, the more manageable rats seem. I start a quiz to make them less scary.

What are their babies called?

Cubs?

Neh-eh. Wrong answer.

Rat . . . lets? I turn my thumb down.

Brats! shouts Em from the kitchen.

Genius, but wrong, I say. *It's* pinkies! They find that funny and we watch videos. Jay thinks they look like willies and that can't be unseen. Actually, it's kind of disgusting, all those bald wee things wriggling together.

Is that why our wee finger's called a pinkie? Elle asks. I'd never thought of that.

Maybe . . . or could be the other way round.

You stalk in from the kitchen with horror hands and go, *Aye, but did you know they also eat their young?* Once they see you're not angry anymore, they squeal, and you let them jump all over you for a bit before settling them in Dee's room. After they're tucked in you come back through and pad the gap between the heater and the fireplace with cushions. That's too much for me, somehow, out of everything, so I head to bed.

I'm nodding off when you come through. I want to tell you about the first time I saw one, until I remember I'm not really talking to you yet. I must have been three. I'm standing next to mum as she chats to the neighbour in the back garden. There's something emerging from the gap at the bottom of the step their feet are on, but they're too far above to notice. It's a wee furry head with a twitching pink nose. I remember pointing at it, mute, for what felt like a long time. How vivid, still, that searching for the word to describe the thing, and I'm feeling all over again the fear that the moment of speaking will pass before I get it out.

Pig, I eventually say, as I try to direct their eyes with my finger. The release of saying it aloud.

Pig. Pig.

Someone must have said rat, because I hold, in my body, that nippy feeling of being corrected. But if you think about it, we'd not long flitted there and I'd only seen real cats and dogs and a few other animals drawn in books. So a pig isn't that far away from a rat. Anyhow, whatever Mum and her pal did there would have been a stooshie and I'd have ended up greeting.

To be fair, there would have been loads of displaced wee creatures birling around the edges of the village. New schemes and motor-ways were getting planted everywhere then. Maybe it was a big mouse, or a vole. Whatever, mum wouldn't have known the differ-ence, and I bet the village blamed us for bringing vermin in our cases from the slums. Anyhow, I don't think you'll appreciate my story from The Land of the Inside Toilet the mood you're in, so you'll never know.

*

Our bedroom yesterday's the last straw. With everything that's been going on I barely register, one, that the cats had held, for a couple of days, a vigil at the charity shop pile under the window; or two, that it had ended. But when TJ comes round, sniffs in the lobby and asks where we're hiding the grow-tent, it clicks. That familiar-unfamiliar cocktail. Sweat? Trainers? Damp? It's been there for days, in everything, and it's starting to swell. God knows how it's taken us so long to acknowledge it. To be fair, we've never got our smell back properly after Covid, but you'd think TJ would know death from his line of work. Or maybe he's like us, still half-noseblind and looking for everything to be all right, despite the evidence. It's like that time, on the doorstep. My nose doesn't have the key yet for the thing in front of it.

This stink's beyond Google though, and you'd need to know the answer already to type in the question. It's seeping into everything and not going away, and Dee could come home any day now, so we're in that moment when we're the only grown-ups in the house.

After TJ's away, I say that there's something in the corner. You sigh, *C'mon then*, and rub your head like you've known it all along. We put our shoes on and I bring the brush and shovel from the kitchen. We prod bags and cushions and clothes and listen, after each poke, like a bomb disposal team.

It's you who sees it first. When you kick the bottom of the stack, something flops down with a jumble of old shoes. There's the weirdest simultaneous slow-motion/blink of an eye, a rigid blur of fur, and you, turning, like some kind of Jackie Kennedy trying to get out of the back of the limo then remembering you're actually the driver. The stench soars up from the collapsed pile and hits hard. Undeniably death. It's like all the other death-whiffs I've encountered in my life have been bottled and released from a single toxic capsule. There's this intense series of split-second memory-premonitions and . . . stacked palettes in the warehouse . . . hide and seeking in the back lanes . . . dozing in ravey armpits in fields . . . bins out the back of the hospital . . . smoking in the rain by the river . . . we're retching – you with the brush and me with the shovel – holding our plastic lances in front of us like two blind knights. Everything's telling us this is a dead thing, but the backs of our necks aren't convinced.

How I move my hand to shift the shoes I've no idea, but you've gone out of your body to some other place where your feet are wee and bare. I shouldn't be smirking at your performance, but I am because I hate you a bit just now for not just fucking dealing with it, Mr I'm-So-Smart. Then you're shouting, *You didn't grow up with it.* I close my ears to your shite and say that we just have to get on with it or it'll just lie there. And that's who we are now, two people with nothing to hear from each other, nudging a stinking wee carcass onto a dustpan. To be fair, you do manage to dunt it into the body-bag I've set up on the floor.

Nothing's alive in there, but the smell has a life of its own. I gag and push the edges over the rat. I double-wrap it inside a biodegradable food bag, which makes no sense as the one inside it's plastic. The cats are back, sniffing. You swipe the brush and tell them they had their chance, but they're already walking away.

They don't need a smartphone to work out it's beyond eating. It's almost funny.

It's so good to get out in the night air. We smoke a spliff and start to breathe again as we walk. I carry the bag until the other side of the park and in silence we jam it into a street bin, because you couldn't leave that in the midden. Then we're giggling like we've scored a point off someone. It'll be hoaching here tomorrow. We look around in case we've been spotted from the big houses, but there's absolutely no-one around. Hardly a light on. It's kind of creepy here, I think, and you ask, *Where are all the cars?*

*

We smell it as soon as we open the close door, so the minute we're in I google **Bicarbonate of soda and vinegar** (of course) and **bleach**. I double-mask and get stuck into the corner. We've plenty blue gloves left over and I wear two pairs. You're right: you never know about Weil's disease. Or fleas. Although they now think it might have been human fleas that carried the plague. It's the vilest thing I think I've ever had to do. I'm not sure you'd have come home if I hadn't said I'd deal with it.

Silver lining, the corner's got us sort of talking again. You message from the bath – **What's the collective noun for a group of rats?**

I reply – **I know this**, but after a few minutes it doesn't come to me so I ask for a clue.

Begins with m. It doesn't help.

Don't tell me yet . . .

But you're still not yourself, and I'm shook too. All night we're like a pair of owls, turning our heads towards every creak. *Maybe it's Em's little friend*, you say. *Fuck, maybe there's more of them.*

It's crossed my mind too, to be honest, so we turn the telly down, stand for a bit and listen to the bags she's left in the hall. Nothing, but in that lull, a weird feeling that the building's scratching its skin, softly, from the inside out. *Don't worry*, the pest control guy told me at the old flat. *They wee black beetles are in every tenement. It's your bare floorboards.* He'd come round to spray after I poured bleach down a crack to kill one that was mooching at the cat food bowl. We didn't have mobiles for memory then, but I'll never unsee how they swarmed up as if on fire. He told me that would keep them away for a bit, but they'd come back, eventually.

Sometimes the solution's as bad. If you poison the rats, you kill the cats who eat them. And during lockdown gulls ate pigeons. No human food scraps to keep them going. TJ sent me a truly gruesome photo of a hollowed-out bird near _____ Square. That was the first time I thought we might never get out of the pandemic. It reminded me of this film I saw about an ultra-religious community where they weren't allowed to take a life, so they would take murderers out to the middle of a loch, tie a fish to their head and keep them afloat. They'd row away and leave them bobbing there, waiting for their winged executioners to divebomb for lunch and smash past the fish to the brain. So only beaks and skulls, not commandments, were broken.

It comes to me. **A mischief of rats!**

You ask if I looked it up.

*

When Em phones, my stomach jumps. The council's been round. They've caught three in traps and think there might be more. I start to think, maybe you're right, there's something bigger going on here. I put her on speaker to save me telling you after. The whole street's hoaching so they told her to bung up any gaps and not to leave the baby alone in a room. My stomach sinks. Two nights was enough, you in a mood and the kids all greeting. No way we can put them up again, when you're sitting at the table with both your hands over your face.

So we're going to Mum's, she sobs. I tell her that'll be nice, and she thinks I'm being sarcastic, which I am, so I pretend I actually mean it. You're mumbling something to yourself as if I'm not here. I ask you what you're saying. Your hands slide down your face.

This is it. I've been telling you. They're running it down to clear us for another one of their fresh starts. I think about saying that the old place was a slum and needed flattening, but I can't be arsed to be honest. You're all about the conspiracies.

This time next year it'll be crawling with students round here, you say as I head to the bedroom. It's freezing with the window up.

Always so bleak you are. And angry. You follow, still banging on about it, saying I refuse see what's going on. We're cornered. They're letting vermin urine soak into the foundations until there's no saving any of it and we'll have to leave. As long as I keep an ear out for when to nod and shake, you'll carry on as if I need converting. But there's no winning because I'm already on your side.

Do you hear me? We might be living with rats but we're not fucking rats, are we? I shake my head. I might not be able to spit it all out like you but knowing you're a human being changes fuck all. In fact, it makes it worse. And there's more than one way to take the piss out of people. It's all very well spouting speeches at me but you're not fucking smart enough to bleach the floor or sweep up the crumbs or keep the lids from falling off. And look where that's got us, Mr Enemy-of-the-rodents. How about you and everyone else round here make it less comfy for them?

I must have forgotten to nod because you're tapping my forehead with your knuckles. I never should have told you how I voted.

So, we're sitting in thirty years of silence when they come round for their stuff, but you play uncle and stretch out your arms for them to dangle from. They punch their wee fists into your stomach to see how strong you are. When you carry their bags downstairs your footsteps tell me they've cheered you up. You're even better when Dee facetimes and says he'll be home at the end of the week. He's having a ball.

He should never come back.

*

You head to bed before me. I hear you moving around. You're in and out of drawers and the wardrobe, but don't ask me to help you find whatever it is you're looking for.

When I come through you get up because you can't sleep, so I watch the news and scroll. There's talk of a run on the pound. That's a worry. YouTube suggests a video of a lab rat – all white and clean with pink eyes – driving a see-through plastic car. Nothing like the monsters round here . . . Anyhow, turns out if you put them up in super-comfy **Disney cages** and reward them with Frooty Loops, they can be trained to drive. Some even like it so much they do it for free. Mad. Scientists call the ones from standard cages **Uber-rats** – because they're passengers (not because they're superior). Anyhow, their **poop contains significantly increased levels of stress hormones** and they can't drive, or do anything extraordinary. People aren't animals, but it's interesting. When I google **uber rats driving**, I get **Showing results for uber *eats* driving**. You'd find that funny.

*

You didn't have to sleep on the couch though. The bicarb and vinegar got rid of the smell. Anyhow, I know when you sneak past the bedroom and out the door that you've had enough. I get to the window in time to catch you scurrying along the street, up the hill, with the big rucksack on your back. The fear of me spotting you is making you hunched. I throw up the sash and lean out to scream something shitty after you, but you don't deserve it. When you're halfway up, you straighten, and I lose sight of you in a surge of people, greyed out in the rain.

I check my phone. **07:33**. It seems later. I check the forecast. **09:00 heavy rain and strengthening wind.**

No way I'm going in after all this. I close the window and lean my cheek against the pane. It quivers every time the close door bangs. Below, there's the usual morning people, all warped through glass and grime. How did it get so dirty?

Weirdly, though, there are whole families heading off towards the station like it's Fair Friday or something. Unfair Friday. You'd laugh at that. Then there's someone on crutches, a cat in a carrier being belted into a back seat and Kay from the ground floor in her jammies with her zimmer, all leaving in cars. A hackney pulls up and TJ stumbles in with his phone to his ear. My gut clenches and I step back from the window as if that'll make things clearer. A notification pops up from The Wee Man, then another, but I don't know what to tell him. Em's phoning and I want to look at you and roll my eyes.

There's too many to count now, down there. Fifty maybe, scattering out of closes and scampering to the main road from side streets, as if they know there's somewhere else they should be.

Behind me, there's a soft thud. Something snuffles, closer, and the hairs on the backs of my hands prickle like whiskers. You'd hate this.

Nicole Le Marie
LAST DAY AT EAST WEMYSS

Yer eroding round the edges
    drizzle fading tae greying waves, a tae alive sea
    fierce, naw friends naw foes
        spume and foam as fallen blossom
    ye stare it down, like ye dae most things
like ye will the end itself, not hunting fossils
anymore, watching as the Picts themselves might
    my son, before the *umah* holding up quartz
        the Cullinan Diamond against the haw
    fingers carmen wi barnacle cuts, numbed clean wi salt
secrets in the silt, roots awe the Lepidodendron.

Pippa Little
BROWN NIGHTS

Last summer, late, I filled your tea cup,
bone and gold, with melted wax:
it sits in its saucer now, lit
pale rose, sets corners fluttering
as my breath teases the wick –

February dark is fields and fields long,
from this sill to the whin ridge and beyond,
wet as a dog's nose, curious
where flame ticks against glass,

wanting only a warm –
out there owl outflies a bullet
and stones stir to ease their aching.
All-invisible: yet I can't draw closed the curtain.

Brown nights and days these are,
slow as peat water snarled
in roan pipe and stell, a calling
far across the valley toward a ship of light

tomorrow I will let soil fill the trails
in both my hands: for now, this window lit
with your small pulse is single thing enough
to bare against the dark.

Marcas Mac an Tuairneir
BANRIGH BHAILTEAN

Fhad 's a seatlaig an duslach am bruthainn maidne,
tha amharc nam fireannach air a' mhalairt làitheil,
cuiridh mnathan-taighe tost air an cainnt chlosta
is an sùilean a' coimhead bho chùl fhalach trìd-dhealrach.

Le mnathan air gach taobh, tha a fola pàrras-uaine,
sgeadaichte le aodach òir, a cho-fhreagras a falt,
ruadh is an òrdugh, àrd fa ceannabhart barra-chaol.

'S sin a tharraingeas sùil an reiceadair don ghrèin,
a leang seachad oirre is tar-sgàil meatailt na h-uinneige,
mus glacar aire le tàladh làimhe maisichte

A' faoisgneadh bho steach-bhathar sìoda, air a dhlòth.
Spreagaidh a gluasad cagairean *Hayret! Oha!*
osnaidhean fo chochaill beusachd agus triutan gàire
aig fir fiosraichte air na tha na laighe fodhpa.

Nì an leadaidh lùbadh gus an dubh-ìochdar a sgrùdadh
am broinn poit *terracotta*, a' gobachadh na h-oir, tha an
sùilean is stiùirichean a' tomhas a' ghaoir-theas làn burmaid,
mus teàrn iad, air an slaodadh air ais

A-steach don dorachdas. Rogsalana na seasamh, sàmhach,
a' feitheamh ceann a-mhàin a bhriseas an àile,
aodann is dath *canteloupe* air, gun fhaicinn san t-*souk*
fad mìle bliadhna,

Ag èirigh air dromannan finic-chnàmhlaich a chinnidh,
an leacadh socharach mu chrìochan an t-soithich, gu dearbh,
's aithne dhan *harem* caran nam ban, is Suileiman
an dùil ri dìnnear giomaich.

QUEEN OF CITIES

As the dust rises in the morning swelter, the men,
overseeing the day's bartering, part, hushed tones
halted by the female retinue, their eyes, cast
beyond the diaphanous veil.

Flanked on both sides, her robe is paradise green,
embellished with cloth of gold, and offsets her
russet hair, piled high beneath her headdress,
tapered into an apex.

This draws this stall's vendor's eye towards the sun,
its arc beyond her and the crosshatch of the
metal-clad window, before his gaze is enticed
by the manicured hand

Emerging from the swathes of imported silk.
Her gesture induces whispers of *Hayret! Oha!*
sighs sheathed with modesty, the men chuckle
knowing what lies beneath.

The lady stoops to scrutinise the obscured depths
of a terracotta pot, poking above the rim, their eyes
and antennules test the wormwood-scented haze,
then descend, dragged,

Back into darkness. Roxelana stands in silence,
awaits a lone head to breach the atmosphere,
its face of cantaloupe hue, unseen in the souk,
for a millennium,

Ascendant on the backs of its jet-shelled kin, their
obliging tessellation around the vessel's confines, yes,
the harem knows a woman's wiles, Suleiman expects
lobster for dinner.

CLÀR AODAINN

mar chuimhneachan air Vito Russo

Dheàlraich lionsaichean a speuclairean, mòr,
an aghaidh an t-saoghail dhùinte a thill iad,
spleuchd a shùilean dubha drilseach air ais tron
tuaileas, a' sàthadh fhathast priobadh criomagan
bhideo nan ochdadan a ghlèidheas amharc,

        oir chunnaic e, air an là a labhair e fìrinn
ro chamara, mar a chì sinn a-nis, a ghàirdeanan,
uaireannan rag mar mhaidean-phiogaid, uair
eile, mar amhaich eala, don dàn suaineadh ris
na th' aig mo leithid, a bhilean –

        làn, is tiugh mar *chaise longue* a bu chofhurt
do a leannan, a dhealaich gus an drannadh e
riutha fhiaclan

        an aghaidh clàr aodann stàit is a miann a
buil air a chumail am falach is fo sgàil, ach b'
aodann àrd-ùrlar, air an do choisich draothan
air bùird uaisleachd a chruthaich e, a chaidh
fodha, cho domhain ri slocan a ghruaidhean,
ga bhàthadh le bhìoras air nach do bhruidhinn
ach esan

        gus an do dh'fhàg faclan fìrinn a bheul.

IN THE FACE

in memory of Vito Russo

The lenses of his glasses gleamed large, against
the closed world they reflected, his eyes, black,
brilliant stared through the haze, pierce still
the flicker of the eighties VHS footage which
enshrines his gaze,

for he saw, on the day he spoke to camera,
as we see now, the truth, his arms, sometimes
rigid like picket sticks, others, like the neck of
a swan, were born to entwine with arms like
mine, his lips –

full, and plump like a chaise longue, were
comfort to his lovers, parted to bare his teeth

in the face of the state that sought to
condemn him to the shadows, but his face was
a stage, on which wastrels trod the boards of
dignity he fought to create, sank deep as his
cheeks collapsed like ground holes, engulfed
by the virus of which only he would speak

until he could speak this truth no more.

ᓴᓐᓇ

mar chuimhneachan air Kelly Fraser

A-muigh air feadh tundra na h-Artaige,
sheirm d' òrain ann am fònaichean-làimh
is coimpiutairean-uchd, far an do dh'èist
feadhainn crùbte fo chanabhas,
a' greimeachadh an t-seann-nòis
is chuala iad ath-innleachadh an cànain
fhad 's a shìn fàin làithean an Earraich
beagan a bharrachd.

Bha feadhainn eile ann an taighean-fiodha is ionadan bailteil
a phuingicheas a' mhòr-rathaid, ag èisteachd
airson na ciad uarach do ghuth
air a chluinntinn air clàr.

Na sampallan
                                        geàrrte
mus an d' ràinig na cùird
aona-cheann   deireannach
is iad, mar do chuid smuaintean,
air an claonadh is ath-chluich *ad infinitum*,
d' inntinn ag ath-thilleadh
gu làraich ciùrraidh.

Tha mi ga chluinntinn an nis an *Sedna*,
onair do ghutha
gun chàireadh *autotune*,
ann am bhideothan tha thu clisgeach
is do shùilean dùinte gus

an saoil mi, anns na mòmaidean seo,
am b' ann don cheòl
a ghèill thu
no duibhre do d' òran,
air a shoillseachadh, mar a liùg e
thar d' fhaire is a stiùir thu,
aig a' cheann thall, air falbh.

ᓯᓚ

in memory of Kelly Fraser

Out, across the Arctic tundra,
your songs rang out of mobile phones
and laptops, where listeners,
some huddled under canvas,
and clinging to the old ways,
heard their language reinvented
as the spring-time daylight
stretched a little longer.

Others, in the wooden houses of urban centres
that punctuate the Highway, listening
for the last time your voice
was heard on record.

The samples

                                    chopped
before the chords might reach
their final   climax
and they, like your thoughts,
warped and replayed *ad infinitum*,
your mind rewinding its way back
to sites of trauma.

I hear it now in *Sedna*,
the honesty of your voice,
unfixed by autotune,
in videos you flinch
and close your eyes and

I wonder, in these moments,
if it was to the music
you succumbed or
the darkness to your song,
illuminated, as it crept across
your horizons and, ultimately,
led you away.

AON GHAOL

às deidh Ariana Grande, 22mh den Chèitean 2017

Chan eil i air ainmeachadh,
ach nuair a bhrùth e an toireannair
gus dà theaghlach air fhichead a chur fo bhròn
spreadh rudeigin na broinn.
      Dh'fhaoidte
gum b' ann am Malabù no an Cathair nan Ainglean
a thug i bhuaipe a speuclairean-grèine, ga dalladh leis an t-solas,
ri sgeing far na ballachan, ach mi an dùil gun do dhùisg sin i
rè na h-oidhche,
      an sgeun, casan nan deugairean nan deann-ruith
      slighe a-mach às an dubh-choimeasg, gan sgaoileadh
      measg na bha, aon uair, nan sgalan gràdhachaidh.
Dh'fhaoidte gun leigeadh i bhuaipe am maidhc
a' gèilleadh don ghuth sin, a' guradh ann an
cnapadh na muineal, cràdh a h-uilnean,
am bad as duirche den toinisg, ag innse
frith-leum dhi –
      truis a-mach.
      Seach sin, tharraing i
      an gasgan-gruaige beagan na b' àirde,
      a' faireachdainn a ciabhan ma guailnean,
san dealachadh,
is ri leth-cheud mìle
dh'fhosgail i a beul, ri òran
is sheinn iad leatha.   Aon ghaol,
                   aon shèist.

ONE LOVE

after Ariana Grande, 22nd May 2017

She does not name him,
but when he pressed the detonator
and sent twenty-two families into mourning
something inside her imploded.
      Maybe
it was in Malibu or Los Angeles
she removed her sunglasses, blinded by the
light, bouncing off the mansion walls, the echo,
unheard within that place, I bet it woke her
in the night,
         the fright, the feet of teenagers racing
         to the exit of the chaos, unfolding in what were
         once the screams of admiration.
She could have lain down the mic
succumbed to that voice, niggling
in her crick of the neck, her aching elbows,
the darkest corner of the mind, telling her to
recoil –
         just go away.
         Instead, she pulled
         the ponytail a little higher,
         felt the tresses cascade about her shoulders,
one last time,
and to fifty thousand
she opened her mouth in song
and they sang with her.   One love,
                      one refrain.

Rob McClure
THE GREEN

Miles beyont the cranes of Govan the river jabbles,
skimmer quicksilver dazzly along the surface of its flowing there.
Grass green and dew-droukit by the spire of St Anne's,
filly-tails high in the blue ahint it,
spring's calling card a sundew-web crocus.

The street cobbled and swepit clean.
Trees filter light, sparkle the leaves and a flaff of sparrow!
The girl's bare white legs dangle on her father's chest.
The bangle on her thin wrist chimes in a sunblink.
Don't skelp her.

THE NIGHT

Mirkins, the night wind souched in the stair-fit in pick-black dark.
A tanker-mouthed collie gurred at its own flickering shadow
as a lang-lippit hairy wheeched her hem above her knee.
The wraith bell chimes.

A thuddy baff and a man belly-flaughtered,
the bet-lick left him in a sopping addle-dub,
fist-foundered and whimpering with a striped face.
Polis wheeps walawaying in the night, shrill.
A gliff, sprinting shadow, scuffle of boots,
a fugie peching, teeth chacking,
kenspeckle figure in his hidey-hole of darkle close.
The whole jing-bang and the row-de-dow of the night!
The wraith bell and its afterstang.

Gillean McDougall
PULSE

I should start by telling you that I'm different. Just in case you have any assumptions, and you will. Folk form an opinion of me very quickly, it seems, and I don't leave them in any doubt. More, they are inclined to tell me what they think. It's possible, to be fair, they're just speaking in the silence that follows me around. Not a bad silence. Not the silence after someone says a terrible thing, or leaves one life to begin another, or maybe dies. Not the silence of disapproval, or disavowal, or disgrace. I like to think it's an amicable silence. It is my silence, and I claim it. I have the right to it and the need of it, because trust me, inside my head the noise is considerable. Like what I imagine an ironworks sounds like, or a place where scaffolding is thrown randomly on the ground morning till night. Some weird charnel house of ideas.

I'm only a girl, early twenties, musician. Tall, with long dark hair. Yet the inside of my head is a factory and curling round these infernal noises is the superintendent, my own inner storyteller. It charts my every move, and I suppose if you pressed me to say when it started (as doctors inevitably have), well, it's been the case since my childhood ended when I was fourteen. I am silent around my mother in particular. She was always bad – perverse, intolerable, vexing – but after Dad went there was nothing to restrain her. So I stopped talking to her, too. Yes, I know this is a trope.

The only place I got calm was in the music, it was the only thing that shut off the clamour, so it's just as well it became my life. As a child, I would get lost in it; hours would disappear in violin practice. Then the school upped me to two lessons a week. Then there was Junior Academy in Glasgow on a Saturday morning and then the letter telling me I was going to London. I didn't look back. Trust me, you wouldn't have looked back either.

This was the proper Royal College, where violinists Daniel Hope and Sasha Rozhdestvensky and Alina Ibragimova had studied, and where plaques to Britten and Vaughan Williams jostled with glossy photos of alumni on the walls. It felt obvious and right – why would I ever go home? I became the go-to for house-sitting, plant-sitting, pet-sitting. Buying food or clothes from Saturday morning street markets in strange parts of London, busking on a high street I'd never seen before or playing my violin in a borrowed flat. In every unknown place my sound changed, developed, grew.

It couldn't last forever though, and I had to come back. But session work and weddings gave me enough to rent a tiny flat and just about cover the bills and now I have the trial with the orchestra. I've heard of players going from one trial to another for years, never getting a job. This is my first time, so I don't know what to expect. I kind of do though. Fat Jo, my desk mate, told me one day what she earned. She must spend it all on her difficult kids as she's certainly not spending it on clothes.

*

If you forced me to name a friend, I'd say Fleur. She's one of those Scottish folk who sound English. She's quieter than me, and yet she talks so much more, but it's all very dull. We've both been on trial with the orchestra but she's finishing soon, and some other hopeful will take her place. My trial's been extended. Fleur has cause to hate me now, but she can't even do that with any degree of competence.

'Trial' is a strange word for it, but actually it's quite appropriate. You're on trial for weeks, being judged by a sixty-five-strong jury of your musical peers. Everything's up for scrutiny. Your time-keeping, your personality, your sight-reading, your outfits. Can you keep it up from ten a.m. to ten p.m.? In the coaches that ferry us to out of town gigs, are you Pond Life or Party?

Fleur plays the flute. Well, she would. Feckan English-sounding Fleur on the flute. Why would you warm to an instrument you can't even see while you're playing? A shrill, feeble thing. You need to be a better flute player to get an orchestral seat because there's fewer of them – I'm currently trialling for the underwhelming but numerous 'rank and file.' Worse, it's a second violin vacancy, at the back desk. About as far down the orchestral pecking order as you can get. I'm nearly out the door.

This tension, of course, feeds my internal story. Trying to be on time, trying to be a step ahead, daily practice, looking good. Because I don't say much, they watch me more. The men, as usual. The alpha females try to work out what I'm at. My desk partner, Jo, is not one of these. She has three troubled children and a diabetic husband. Her clothes always look too small, like she's pretending to be someone else.

Our section leader is Dan. Ran Dan. Dan, Dan, the funny wee man. Except he's a bit rakish, and he has three children too and a wife with an Etsy business making lacy bloomers for brides. He wears radge leather boots that should look comic on a guy his age, but he gets away with it. Just after I went on trial, Dan turned round from the front of the section at the start of the rehearsal.

'Roxy,' he said.

I looked at him and waited. He jinked his head around the others sitting in between us.

'I can't see you,' he said. 'Move your chair so I can see you. I always need to be able to see you.'

My face was red as I moved my seat and music stand, and the whole section shuffled round making room. Everyone was smiling at me. Or laughing. 'Phew,' Jo said, 'that's my exercise for the day.'

Fleur has one outfit she wears for every concert. It smells of old damp wardrobe and is a black polo neck dress with long sleeves. She wears black tights and ballet flats. I have lots of concert outfits; in fact, I see it as a challenge to constantly reinvent 'long, black.' Crepe, sequins, velvet, heels, slit, crushed or demure. Even Fleur's bored with saying 'something new?' every time. She said, you'll spend all your trial salary and end up with nothing. Like that's going to happen.

I make sure Dan can always see me now. Another day, he turns round. 'Roxy,' he says, 'do a swap with Lawrence here. Sit by me.'

They're not joking. I knew this might happen. Everyone's smiling – they knew it too. Lawrence does a camp little bow and goes to sit in my seat, where Jo greets him like a long-lost friend. I'm right up front, three feet from the podium. And they're all smiling at me, the violas and the cellos. It's a different view and I like it. The air is purer here.

Dan looks at me. 'Okay?' he says.

This is really when it matters. I check my tuning, wipe my palms on my hankie. I just look at the music and breathe. Concentrate. It's the Kodály *Dances of Galánta*, and I know it inside out. It's a big play for the strings, but I nail it and think I've done well; I hope they think so too. I need this job with a neediness that's beyond needing, if you see what I mean. When Dan lets me go back to my seat, Fleur's watching me and smiling her thin smile. A real flute kind of smile.

*

We're off on tour. Playing the Royal Albert Hall in London, always a highpoint for what they call in their brochures 'regional' orchestras. Nothing prepares you for the size of the place, the huge dome with its flying saucer acoustic panels, the movement of the air, the clarity of sound. It's near my old college, so I'm on comfortable ground and everyone feels light. Fun and games. No matter what instrument, Pond Life or Party, we're all on our mettle, even the guys who stayed up late drinking in the hotel. What happens on tour stays on tour.

The new conductor for these concerts will be our assistant next season. He has a funky, underfed look like an Eastern European ice skater, and long blond hair. You know these people who look spindly until you're standing next to them and they're made of iron. Sometimes when he makes a big gesture, beads of sweat fly from him like he's just pulled off a triple Salchow and landed well. He's given me the talk occasionally, no action. I know he's got a wife and a baby. Notches on the stick.

It's an all-Beethoven programme; overture then piano concerto in the first half. After the interval, I'm last to leave the green room. In the corridor by the stage there's the maestro waiting for us all to go on. He's chugging water and throwing back pills from a blister pack. He sees me and does a comedy wave with the box of paracetamol. I laugh and keep walking.

We take our seats and then the leader comes on, gets his applause, sits down and we tune to the 'A' from the oboe. A wine-y smell comes from the audience and the atmosphere is brilliant, the bright lights, the Radio 3 announcer speaking into a lip mic in his box. Dan turns and gives us all his best smile, we're coasting to the end now with Beethoven's *Pastoral*. Triple Salchow comes on, takes his bow, turns to us, runs his hand through the blond. He doesn't like a podium. He likes to be on a level with us, and he doesn't use a score. Everything's in his head. That's a lot of affectation, but he owns it.

The first movement goes well. Jo gives me a smile as some fan always applauds before they should. Salchow mops his face with his handkerchief – he's sweating a lot but it's a hot night. He's preparing himself for the long slow *Andante*, we all are. It's such a lovely extended thing, the movement old Beethoven called 'scene by the brook.' We're all preparing. Lovely, lovely. He raises his arms and closes his eyes.

And then he goes down. Heavily, in the pause between the upbeat and the down. The stage cloth absorbs the sound and a flurry of tiny dust motes sparks into the bright light. It's like he's fallen from the cross to the floor in front of us and he's not moving. There's a collective gasp and the air in the hall shimmers.

Then the front desks are round him, passing their instruments back, moving chairs. Everyone's round him, the backstage staff are out now and a guy from the BBC wearing headphones talking into a handset. Jo is whispering 'ohmygod ohmygod ohmygod' and it's too close for me, I know how this ends. I rest my fiddle on my thigh and just look at the music. Bar one. *Andante molto mosso*. Twelve-eight time signature, not many of those around. I follow the notes on the page and the Beethoven starts in my head, a slow murmuring. The beats of my heart press under my shirt.

They carry him off, clumsily and heavily; for such an elegant boy, he makes a bad dead weight. Everyone sits down, the hall manager makes an announcement and the BBC guy scurries back to his box. It's over, and first our leader goes off and then we follow. The audience don't know what to do; there's a faint ripple of inappropriate applause.

In the green room, they're working on him in a corner, and they've found a doctor (these audiences are never short of a few) who's fisting his chest and counting 'and one and two and three and four and . . .' That's what really does it. That's my voice at fourteen, Dad on the kitchen floor, the phone jammed to my ear, counting and fisting. Jesus, people are muttering, what age is he? Fleur starts dismantling her flute, shaking droplets of saliva on to the floor.

Jo thrusts a bottle of water at me and I'm glad of it, gulping it down as I put my violin in its case, wrapping it in the silk scarf. Ambulance crew come and take the boy away, but I know he's gone, his waxy face behind the oxygen mask. They do that for other people's benefit. A hand on the back of my neck, hot, heavy, makes me jump.

'Okay, Roxy?' Dan's going round his section, a touch on the shoulder, a reassuring word. We've another concert tomorrow, rehearsal at ten, they're phoning round for a dep. See you in the morning.

'What are you doing now?' Fleur says and I bat her away like a fly.

Outside a fine summer drizzle's come on, a smirr of rain gives the Albert Hall the look of a stage-set in the gloom; ghostly, not really there. It's a hot evening and the rain steams as small groups of players mingle with the audience finding their way home. I need to walk back to the hotel, get distance. Recalibrate, forget all that, be in myself, concentrate, focus. I struggle with my umbrella, my fiddle case, my bag. Someone calls my name.

'Roxanne.'

Oh, will you all go away and leave me in peace, you people and your upper-cultured shit. Because walking this road is hard, right? Hard and long and lonely. I dip the umbrella, squinting in the rain. Dan's by the kerb holding open the door of a black cab.

'Want a lift?'

He's looking at me uncertainly, this man who should know better. The noise in my head quietens. That's how it happens, how we make choices. Or it's how I make them. Life can change in a moment; in a beat, like a heartbeat. In that silence between the upbeat and the down. The pause, the pulse. Pulling down the umbrella, I shake the rain from it and walk towards the cab. The water drops fly away like stars.

Crìsdean MacIlleBhàin
A' GHÀIDHLIG

I.

Tha 'n cànan seo mar bhoireannach, is miann
cho anabarrach mòr air leanabh aice,
air an t-sìol fhaireachdainn a' dol an tiughad
ann an doimhne a cuim, agus an dèidh

saothair spreachail 's cràdh uile na breith
(a bha cur eagal oirre cuideachd, ged
nach b' ann gu leòr gus a mì-mhisneachadh!)
cùbhraidheachd 's maoith' a naoidhein a mhealtainn,

air cho gleadhrach a ghearan is a ghul,
sinean a cìochan a' fàs teannaicht', rag
le pailteas bainne 'son a bheathachaidh –
gus na ràinig a mì-fhoighidinn

ìre 's nach robh i miarraideach a thaobh
athar, sloinnidh no eadhon ainm – rinn i
mo roghainn fhìn, 's nar dithis fhuair sinn gineal
fallain, tairbeartach is cuideachd dreachmhor.

II.

'Cha do lorg sinn fiù 's facal nur dàintean
air a' Ghàidhealtachd, air tìr nam beann,
nan gleann 's nan gaisgeach, no air eachdraidh allail
nan saighdear an seirbheis na h-ìompaireachd,

na h-ìobairtean a rinn iad, is an dìlse
do bhan-righinn an Lunnainn. Cha tuirt thu
dad air na h-Innse Gall, air croit no feannaig,
air fèileadh-beag no cèilidh, crodh no monadh.

Ciamar a dhearbhar leat gur dàintean Gàidhealach
a th' ann, 's naoimh Chaitligeach a' nochdadh annta?'
'Air cho danarra 's a nì sibh m' àicheadh,
bha mi gam ghineamhainn bho 'r leasraidh fhèin

's ma bhitheas grèidheadh Èireannach san tràth,
ciod e an diofar? Nach robh na drùth-mhic
an-còmhnaidh na bu smioraile is neartmhoir'
na clann an lagha? 'S na bu dhreachmhoir' cuideachd?'

III.
Feumaidh iad tuigsinn, ma tha iad ag iarraidh
gum mair a' Ghàidhlig anns an àm ri teachd,
gum bu chòir dhi gach comharradh a th' aice,
na rudan àbhaisteach a thug dhi caractar

's nàdar a thrèigsinn. Fàs 'na leòmhann-làir.
Coimheadaidh sin mar chealgaireachd no brathadh,
mar chall gach luach 's eileamaide prìseil.
Nach b' fheàrr gu robh an cànan air seargadh

gu tur, na fhaicinn falamhaicht', a' traoghadh?
Mì-dhealbhaichte? Ach feumaidh sibh mo chreidsinn:
chan eil dòigh eil' ann air a leasachadh
ach gun tèid e 'na àite bàn, làn-choltach

car sealain ris a' chreutair a ghoideas
dath nan oibseactan ris am bi e beantainn.
Ath-lorgar leinn mu dheireadh thall gach feart
a b' annsa, taisgt' gu sàbhailte 'na bhroinn.

IV.

Aig an toiseach bha mi smaoineachadh
gun rachainn a-steach do shaoghal na Gàidhlig
gus gach fiamh is luach a bh' ann ath-aithris,
mar bheathach ann an àit'-ionaltraidh ùr

is ged nach bi na lorgas e de fheur
is luibhean ann ro bhlast' a-rèir a bheachd,
's a stamagan ag iarraidh ùine gus
am fodar ùr a chnàmhadh leis gach searbhaig

fheumail, fàsaidh e mu dheireadh thall
cleachdte riutha. An àite sin, bha mi
'g ath-chuimseachadh a' chànain air mo rùintean
mar gum b' e criadh a bh' ann, a dh'ùisnichinn

gus ìomhaigh dhealbhachadh air m' aogas, air
mo ghnàthannan is m' fhidreachdainn. Dè 'n seòrsa
toibheum a choilean mi? An tèid mo choinneal-
bhàthadh air a sgàth aig a' cheann thall?

V.

A chànain, 'nam shùilean tha thu nad organ
anabarrach aibheiseach, nach deach
oisnean ciana 's pìoban diurraiseach
uidheim thoinnt' a rannsachadh chionn bhliadhnan.

'S mo dhànarrachd a' cinntinn, bidh mi feuchainn
'n dàrna bhùird-iuchrach, is an treasa fir,
mo chasan a' gluasad thar nan casachan
le luathas nach dèan ach sìor fhàs nas braise.

Bidh 'n t-organ mar lìon rathad-iarainn air
nach robh ach na loidhnichean àbhaisteach
gan cleachdadh, is na trèanaichean a-nis
a' ruighinn àitean anns nach fhacas siubhlaich'

's nach cualas sgiorrghail beur na fìdeig ait
an cuimhne duine beò – dùisgidh i plapail
is sgiathalachadh am measg na h-eunlaith diombaich
tha 'g àiteachadh druim-bhoghannan na h-eaglais'.

VI.

Ma bheanas mi ri roinnean den bhòrd-iuchrach
nach robh gan cur gu feum ro fhad', ciod iad
na h-èifeachdan a leanas? Ann an doire
dubharach nam pìob, bidh nead beag, blàth

luchagan air an riastradh, is cluinnear
sgiamhadh sgalanta coltach ri notan
nam feadan as cuinge, bige, eangarra.
Ma dhùisgear fuaimean canranach an roinn

as doimhne, bidh cat air barra-bhalla àrd
a' smaoineachadh gur crònan fogharach
a shinnsir ana-mhòir a bhruadair e
a th' ann, 's an uairsin nochdaidh e a h-ìnean,

deas ri ruaig a chur air creutair ùr –
luchd-èisteachd beag air beag a' cruinneachadh
fo ioghnadh ann an corp na h-eaglaise,
cuid chreidmheach, cuid nach eil ach feòrachail.

Christopher Whyte
GAELIC

I.

This language resembles a woman overwhelmed
by such a powerful longing to have a child,
to experience the seed thickening
deep inside her body, and after

all the pain and travail of giving birth
(which also made her afraid, but not
sufficiently for her to get discouraged)
to enjoy her infant's fragrance and softness

however noisily it cried and complained,
her nipples getting tight and rigid
with abundant milk to nurture it –
that her impatience rose to a pitch

where she couldn't be choosy about
father, family or even a name – so she
chose me, and together the two of us had
children that were healthy, plentiful and handsome.

II.

'We couldn't find so much as a word in your poems
about the Highlands, the land of mountains,
glens and heroes, or the notable history
of soldiers in the service of the Empire,

the sacrifices they made, or their loyalty
to the Queen in London. You never said
anything about the Hebrides, a croft or a lazybed,
kilts and ceilidhs, cattle or heather moors.

How can you claim that these are Gaelic poems
when even Catholic saints find a place in them?'
'However resolutely you disown me,
I was begotten from your very loins

and if the dish has Irish seasoning,
what difference does that make? Weren't bastards
always tougher and more resolute
than lawful children? As well as being more handsome?'

III.
They have to understand that if they want
Gaelic to have a future, then it must
relinquish all the features, all the usual
markers that made up its character

and nature – become a chameleon.
That may look like treachery or deception,
the loss of every valued element.
Wouldn't it be preferable if the language

withered away, than seeing it emptied, drained?
Deformed? You have to take my word for it:
the only way it has of moving forward
is to become a blank, similar

for a while to the animal which steals
the colours of the objects that it touches.
The qualities that we loved best in it
will re-emerge in the end, undamaged, safe.

IV.

To begin with I imagined
I'd enter the world of Gaelic so as to
Imitate every tone and value I encountered
like a beast brought to new grazing ground

and even if it doesn't find the grass
or the plants there particularly tasty
and its stomach requires time in order
to digest the new fodder with the needed

acids, it gets accustomed in the end.
Instead of which, I remodelled
the language to my own intentions
as if it had been clay that I was using

to make an image of my face,
my ways and feelings. Was what I did
blasphemous? Am I going to be
excommunicated because of it?

V.

Language, in my eyes you are an amazingly
extensive and complex organ, fitted out
with distant corners and secret pipes
no one has explored for ages back.

As I get braver, I start investigating
the second keyboard, and then the third,
my feet constantly picking up speed
as they move back and forth across the pedals.

The organ is like a railway network
of which only the habitual lines were in use
while now there are trains running
to places where no one has seen a traveller

or heard the shrill peal of a happy whistle
in living memory – it provokes fluttering
and flapping of wings from the indignant
birds that inhabit the vaults of the church.

VI.
If I touch parts of the keyboard
that have long been out of use, what
will be the effect? Amidst the shadowy
thicket of the pipes, in a small, warm

nest mice get startled, and you hear
a high-pitched squealing like the notes
of small, narrow, nimble whistles.
If the grumbling tones of the deepest ones

awaken, a cat on a high rafter
thinks he can hear the resonant purring
of the enormous ancestor in his dreams
and bares his claws, getting ready

to give chase to some new animal –
little by little wondering listeners
gather in the body of the church,
some of them pious, others merely curious.

Mora Maclean

THE HYPO-WITCH

Skewered back awake by shriek:
that jarring elongation of my name;
the punctured dark illuminating *3:13 a.m.*

My body panicked into padding barefoot,
dead-legged down the hall – to find her
wearing you: that same floral modesty,

salt-and-pepper, flyaway hair, an old woman's
slackened slippers beside the bed – fooling no-one.
Eyes flicker feral, side to side, register

me as peripheral to even this small hour,
then close and open – each time in cartoon
disbelief – as if you're still somewhere

in there, aghast at an off-kilter room, or trying
to blink her gone. It'll take me stood over
the crone trying to spin things out on your bed:

her clenched refusal of glucose, sips of milk
-cooled, sugared tea; my stance of insistence
on every gnash and swallow of the back-up carbs.

Once I've pricked your thumb for blood to bead,
clocked the risen level by the gadget's dim digits,
I'll wash you of her foul, soiling ways; for now,

gone clammy, you shudder, gums chittered in spite
of the duvet swaddling your frame, her wizened
grip dying back along every sweetened vein.

The whole performance replaying, as I lie – woken
to you several years gone, and her in her small-hours
element, crowing; with no way to bring you home.

Kevin MacNeil

FALL IN LOVE AND BUY A HORSE

'It's half giraffe, half anteater, half horse, half deer and half some more giraffe.' The man crouches, leans over the dark mass, prods it with a hesitant finger. 'And definitely dead.'

Macy Starfield bends down beside the stranger and regards the heavy black shape on the pavement, her forehead wrinkling in disbelief and pity.

'I mean, what was it?' says the man.

*

Shall I buy a new book, she thinks, or a carbon monoxide alarm? In her thirty years on this Earth, she's read eleventy squillion books. She loves the vicarious experiences they give her. She has travelled to other planets, razed cities to the ground, sought enlightenment, shot a great many deserving men. Perhaps, she muses, there is a story out there about carbon monoxide that is so compelling it makes you immune to CO poisoning. *That* is how life should be.

Macy puts the laptop down on the coffee table in front of her and stands, her lower back momentarily flaring as she straightens. Her breath clouds in the icy air of her flat. Macy's feet are like corpses in sleeping bags; her hands, now that she has stopped hammering at her keyboard, are already growing icily painful in their fingerless mittens. Like silence, the evil cocoon of cold and damp seems to emphasise her loneliness. She walks feeling back into her feet by padding in slow, heavy rectangles around the living room like one of those mindful monks – only, if her mind is full of anything it is full of sadnesses and self-criticism and choruses from songs she hates. Instead of earworms, why can't she have text-worms, where profound and eloquent insights from great authors come alive unbidden in her head instead?

Mind you, Macy has concluded that absorbing so many books throughout this life has expanded her self into a much larger and vastly more varied entity than it would otherwise have been. Alas, resulting in a more complex and more miserable self. She envies the happiness of her distant friends who live a simpler life, working in an angst-free supermarket, neatly stacking tins on shelves, facing packages towards the customer in neat rows. Macy was a shelf-stacker herself during her teenage years and still considers that the most satisfying job she's had.

Macy Starfield.

To her fading family she is mouse-quiet, awkward, sullen.

To some friends she is the wittiest person they've met.

To others she is a brooding, humourless, judgemental party-killer.

To alcohol she is a genius and a menace.

To those in her book group she is enviable and invisibly loathed.

I grow tired of exaggerating my part in other people's lives – is a thought that arises in her mind regularly.

Recently her reflections have taken a morbid turn. If I do kill myself, she thinks, and determination has anything to do with it, I shall will myself to come back as a sunflower.

The first condition of happiness – is that how it goes? – is that the link between humanity and nature should not be broken.

Meanwhile she is striving to be good, positive, and caring.

Everything I understand, I understand only because I love.

Well, then I must love, she determines.

Still. She has heard the word 'altruism' spoken out-loud eight times in her life. Has seen it put into practice fewer times than that.

Everyone thinks of changing the world, but no one thinks of changing themselves.

It's so cold in here she decides to take a walk outside, where, counter-intuitively, it might be a safer world for her, outside being, also counter-intuitively, a bigger place than her mind currently is.

*

'I mean, what was it?' says the man.

On this crisp dark autumnal night in the Riverside area of Stirling, officially-a-city-but-really-it's-a-town, in the middle of Scotland, two strangers have tacitly agreed to solve a small mystery. Macy is assessing the guy beside her as much as the dead animal. For him, the question is what this animal was; for Macy, it's how did it die. And also: 'Wait, you've never seen a greyhound before?'

'Is that what it is? Was, rather,' says the man, looking baffled in the anaemic streetlighting. His eyes glint vaguely. 'I've heard of them; I mean, I know what they are.' They both feel what he said fill the air between them with stupidity.

He has the melancholy of a man doing his failing best to battle something unyielding but grim – perhaps illness, or middle-age. But now he disarms Macy with 'Then let's do something about it. The creature's still warm. Ish.' He glances round. He puts a brave face on, to combat the inane remark he made. 'There!' He nods towards the group of shops a few yards up the pavement. There is a newsagent's, a chiropractor's, a veterinary practice, and a dental surgery.

'It's ten at night,' says Macy, shaking her head. 'The vet's closed.'

'No – there!' says the stranger, rising to his feet and rushing along the pavement towards the intermittent blinking of a light on a wall.

Macy is thinking about the flashing light and Morse code and how some strangers are indeed very strange and as she does so she semi-consciously lays a hand on the deceased greyhound – it feels glossy and warm; the hair is thin, and its body heat seems to suggest that the dog died only a little while ago. Seems unfair that such an elegant animal should be dead. It has no collar. Could be micro-chipped? Macy strains to see what the man is wrestling with on the wall—

Oh! A defibrillator. She hasn't seen one in public since she skulked about the skulls and skeletons of the deathly grey catacombs beneath Paris. Bravo, if people have campaigned to start dotting these life-sparker machines around the streets of Scotland.

They get to it, she and the stranger, and perform the nearest thing to a miracle she's ever witnessed . . . they only shock the greyhound back to life!

The greyhound is now breathing by him – Macy looks – no, *her*self. The in-breaths and exhalations are swift and heavy, but not unnatural.

Amazed, Macy and the stranger look at each other for a long moment.

Macy shakes her head, marvelling. 'We did it.'

The stranger blows his cool by trying to be cool: 'Easy peasy lemon squeezy.'

Barely needing a moment to think, Macy outsmarts him: 'Chest-compressed lemon zest.'

He gives a dry, almost confused, laugh. Pauses. 'I don't know what to do with him.'

'Her.'

'Ah, see? You're the expert.'

'We can't leave a resurrected greyhound out here in the street. You gotta car? Take her home with you.'

'I'm homeless,' the man lies.

Macy gives the man her laser-beam stare. 'Uh-huh,' she says. 'Homeless. That's why you're wearing a golf club tie.'

'I have a cat and a wife who's allergic to dogs,' the man lies.

'Why don't you just admit, "My willingness to be kind doesn't actually go that far",' says Macy.

'I think you'd be a good mother – or owner – or whatever – of this dog,' says the man and it is difficult to tell if he is lying, perhaps because what he is saying happens to be true.

'There is no greatness where there is not simplicity, goodness and truth,' says Macy, channelling her beloved Tolstoy to the man, who is now convinced she is batshit crazy.

No matter. Macy, in fact, has already decided that, having brought the greyhound back from the dead, she will now bring it into her life.

*

Later that night she sets out a bowl of water and a dish of plain boiled rice for the greyhound. The internet claims they like rice. She will buy proper dog food tomorrow. Meanwhile the greyhound strikes up a conversation with her. This is how things are.

After gobbling the entire mound of rice in seconds and slurping at the water for about a minute, the greyhound looks around the barely furnished room, gives a snort, and climbs up onto the sofa, where she walks in a circle three times, lies down, stretches out and says: 'So. You gotta name?'

Macy is forced to press against the arm of the couch. 'I, uh, I'm Macy. Macy Starfield. Um – you?'

'I'm Luna the Greyhound.' The dog scans the room. 'Your flat is colder than a fish's heart. Find me a blanket. What do you do?'

'Nothing. I'm nobody. A failed checkout operator turned failed fishing-boat captain turned failed writer.'

'Oh jeez. Someone call the vet. I'm gonna be the first ever dog who was *voluntarily* put to sleep.'

'Talking of vets, you do realise I just brought you back from the dead?'

'I wasn't dead. I was . . . hibernating.'

'And by the way, same question; what do you do?'

'I greyhound.' Luna pauses. 'You gonna buy some kibble – the decent kind, not the cheap stuff – tomorrow? I mean – plain rice on its own? Would *you* eat that?'

'Oh, I'm sorry, what would Her Highness like to eat?'

'For now, I'd even settle for a carrot slathered in peanut butter. Fetch the blanket first. Off you go. Then the peanut butter. And I do mean *slathered*.'

Luna the Greyhound is not grey but black and is the most colourful character a depressed Hebridean woman in Stirling could meet. Even her laziness is helpful. Macy's life takes on a new dimension. Luna the Greyhound sleeps seventeen hours per day, which improves Macy's night-time sleeping pattern as she begins to consider eight hours of sleep a cinch by comparison. The pair eat together, go on meandering walks, read serious papers and literary journals, and watch films while trading smartass comments. Macy and Luna the Greyhound watch *Groundhog Day* every evening until they grow sick of it. They view Gus Van Sant's shot-by-shot remake of Hitchcock's *Psycho* numerous times. They read and re-write verbatim Borges's 'Pierre Menard, Author of the Quixote'.

Luna the Greyhound begins to show more of an interest in Macy's life. One night, she asks Macy, 'If your island was so great, why did you leave it?'

'For the same reason most folk are homesick for the present moment.'

Luna hesitates. 'I – what?'

'Minor hermits go to the wilderness, major hermits go to the city.'

Luna the Greyhound learns that, much like herself, this human has depths.

The winter months draw them into an exponentially closer friendship. Their minds grow more lively.

One famous evening, for example, as Luna the Greyhound reads to Macy, they invent Tolstoy Night. Luna the Greyhound, with an impish glitter in her eyes, recites an excerpt from the diary of Count Lev Nikolayevich Tolstoy, who wrote on the twenty-fifth of January 1851: '*I've fallen in love, or think I have. Went to a party and lost my head. Bought a horse which I don't need at all.*'

Luna the Greyhound slams down the book, launches off the sofa, dizzies herself with room-zoomies, and, panting, plants four hand-sized paws on the floor in front of Macy, tail still a blur. 'Check the date!' says Luna the Greyhound, breathless. 'Twenty-fifth of January! I'm starting an alternative to Burns Night for those with an aversion to haggis and middle-class kitsch. Every January the twenty-fifth everyone will be encouraged to fall in love and buy a horse.'

Macy grins. 'Yes. An unnecessary horse.'

Luna the Greyhound glowers: 'No horse is unnecessary.'

Macy pets her sleek glossy head, nodding, and says, 'There could be speeches loaded with quotations from the old Russian master.'

'Yes! And songs. We'll take the words and make them into songs. *"Everyone thinks of changing the world, but no one thinks of changing themselves."* Or, *"True life is lived when tiny changes occur".*'

They sit, human and greyhound, in loyal silence for a moment, contemplating Tolstoy Night. Macy realises that just like pop music ear-worms, readers' brains can indeed accumulate text-worms, and if one reads well and listens well these can be healthy and beneficial.

Luna the Greyhound does not – and never will – overtly thank Macy for saving her life, as if this whole episode is a test of Macy's decency (an unacknowledged kindness being more powerful than one that is witnessed, publicised, or bragged about).

In the future, they will debate about who saved whom.

And what of the man in the golf club tie who claimed he had a cat and a wife who was allergic to dogs? He did belong to a golf club, and he did have a wife once upon a time, but she has long since divorced him. He works in middle management at a supermarket, and his Saturdays are now and then enlivened by a visit to his football team's grounds. His evenings are empty.

He has not been saved – but he is thinking about salvation. The night he helped rescue a greyhound has taken on a fable-like quality in his mind. He supposes this might be the kind of thing that Japanese novel he read was getting at.

One night in late January, feeling acutely alienated, he urges himself to dream of a resurrected greyhound. Instead, he sees a half-dozen frantic doped greyhounds bursting in fluid cheetah-leaps around a racing track, while he stands hunched at a barrier beside a desultory group of grey-haired men who stare cursing at the dogs with adrenalised animosity, ruing the chances they took and those they did not and, at their most lucid, wondering whether their own life's mechanical lure, money, has not been a fix, a lie, a decoy. He wakes up with an unexpected urge to fall in love and buy a horse and to rid himself of fixes, lies, decoys. But as he moves about his day, the dream wears off, and he begins to doubt everything. He reasons that he will never in this life be able to afford a horse. Instead, he will look into getting a retired greyhound from a charity and he will spend the little money he has today on a carbon monoxide alarm and a new Murakami. He will learn Japanese. He will bring himself back from the dead.

Annie Muir
BELDINA

Bobbing along to Ghost Town,
a girl stops at our table –

There's two songs left on the jukebox
if you want to choose some?

She's alone, drinking scotch and beer,
she talks to everyone, types into her phone,

floats back to the jukebox, and us,
I love old man pubs! Comes here to read

and write poetry. My friend nudges me –
I ask her name. Her friend or boyfriend arrives,

they look at their phones, she dances.
I wave to her across the pub when we leave.

A week later I find her again, online.
She was a singer. I didn't know her.

We sit at her table sometimes,
cheers to the photo of Beldina on the wall.

Chris Neilan
ME AS ME

It begins with me as me, rolling down the passenger side window and turning up the volume. Summer is in the air – you'd smell it if you were here. *I am the world's forgotten boy, the one who searches and destroys.* I wonder what it's like to be a boy. I wonder what it's like to be Iggy Pop, screwing a teenage fangirl on smack. Men can fuck teenage girls, long as they're also a rock star, and not, say, a school teacher, or a Premier League football player.

It begins with me in her car, and her things in the footwell, in the glove compartment: Sublime and No Doubt and Weezer CDs, plastic chipped at the hinge, eyeliner pencils worn to a nub and their shavings dusting the foot mat, empty packets of Skips. She's saying

Oli's meeting us there

and tapping on the wheel. It begins with her as her, there in all her herness, the wisps of blonde hair up the back of her neck, the dry skin on her lower lip under the gloss. Oli'd said

You should see how wet she gets

said it with a gleam, and he'd kissed me on the cheek when he said goodbye, grazed my fingertips with his. *I am the world's forgotten boy*. It begins with tinny guitars spiking in the red and an engine thrumming up Ditchling Beacon, struggling in the gear changes, summer sun falling, and her saying

Oli's meeting us there

and throwing no looks at me, giving no hint of anything. Just tapping the wheel, tapping the wheel, and me as Iggy Pop singing

Baby penetrate for me . . . ow!

and she glances my way to grin.

I didn't see the incident . . . no . . . around ten I think . . . yes, quite a lot of blood.

We pull up on Madeira Drive in time to smoke to the sunset. You can see the line of gold on the sea beginning to thin, or rather we can, me and her. *I am the world's forgotten girl.* But girl doesn't rhyme with destroy. I tell her

Do the manly thing

which means roll a joint, and she says

Aye captain

and takes the tin from her bag. Her bag says COOKIE I THINK YOUR TAME in blue biro between the stitching above the front pocket zip. I added an apostrophe and an e in red, but my red has faded in the rain. Her bag smells of her car: fumes and tobacco, and feet. Oli says

You should see her room

as if I haven't. He says

She loves wearing these little black knickers

as if I didn't give them to her. We sit there, me as me and her as her, on the ledge below the promenade, watching the water, as the warmth begins to fall away from the day. The sea is almost still, the lights on the pier weirdly ethereal. Our feet dangle over the ledge, as we stare down at the concrete below. I ask her

If you *had* to choose a way to die, what would you choose?

and our Converse are kicking the air. The weed is old and dry and catches in our throats. She says

Fucked to death

and we laugh, and the gold line reduces, and the weed creates a tumbling sensation, and I put my head on her shoulder. She strokes my hair. Oli'd said

You should see how wet she gets

and she strokes my hair, strokes my hair. You should *see* how *wet* she gets. You should get down there and look.

I saw him approach, but I didn't see the thing start, so . . . no, I only saw the aftermath . . . well I'd heard the screams, so . . .

A queue of people outside the main door: strappy tops and camo trou and lip piercings and lace chokers, band t-shirts and gelled up hair and skirts over jeans and bracelet beads. People hugging themselves, a breeze from the sea, groups getting stoned on the stones, chugging cans of cider, two boys chasing each other, feet slipping and slanting on the pebbles, laughing high and short-breathed like hyenas, like girls, flush-cheeked, jeans slipping down showing boxers, downy hair on smalls of backs, dark patches under pits. I wonder what it's like to be a boy, chased by a boy, giggling like a girl. She sucks on the roach and the last embers flare gold, and still sucking in she hands it to me, says

Ere y'are

and lets her breath out, and almost no smoke comes. I grip the
roach, damp from her mouth, between finger and thumb, and suck.

*I saw some of it . . . I saw afterwards, when he was standing up and
trying to lift the railing . . . and I saw the paramedic putting pressure
on the wound . . .*

We enter with me as her, her as me. We hold hands. Fingers inter-
twined. The bar area is full of men, pop punk played way too loud
through venue-grade speakers, something about how someone's
mom has got it going on. She says

Bever*age*, Number One?

to rhyme with Taj, as in Mahal, and I say

Aye captain

and her hand uncouples from mine to wave at a t-shirted barman.

Engage

she says, in her Picard voice, as we raise the plastic pints to our
mouths, and the beer is cold and watery, and she looks around,
looks around. And this is where I tell you about The Time.

The Time: I'd taken a knife to my arm and cut too deep. It was on
account of the emptiness in my chest, and all the weed. I'd been
lying in the road in the middle of the cul-de-sac and she'd tied
her socks around the wound (Minnie Mouse ones), and as the
ambulance arrived she'd stood up to flag it down, and I'd said don't
tell my mum.

Keep pressing on it

she'd said, and the ambulance had pulled over, and this man
and woman in their green uniforms got out, and she went to
them and said something before they came over. She sat in the
back of the ambulance with me for the ride to hospital, me lying
on the trolley, her sitting next to it holding my hand, the male
paramedic saying

That's it. Keep your breathing slow and steady. Good. Still feeling
lightheaded? Keep breathing. Good

in this deep calm voice, like a bedtime story, and I feel like maybe
I asked him to

Read me a story

and then laughed to myself for a long time, but then again maybe
that was just in my head.

*I mean people were saying someone was dead, but . . . I think that
was just, like . . . no I didn't really see it actually happen, so I can't
really say . . .*

Oli's there as him: sitting on a table with his feet on a chair and
a hoodie tied around his waist, holding a too-full plastic pint
that slops over the brim as he hops down. He sees her first, but
then he sees me, and looks at me as he hugs her, and I tug at the
cuffs of my long-sleeve. I think about what she'd told me about
his dick:

Kind of curved, like a pirate's sword

and she'd smiled on one side of her mouth.

I don't know, I mean, I saw him falling into the railing, and I guess it came apart . . . I don't know, but my friend said it all happened pretty quick . . . is she all right?

When the band take to the stage the venue's main area is dense and dark and stuffy. Phantasmagoric stage lights strobing over spikes and backcombs. Oli's hand rests on the small of her back, where the vest top and studded belt expose the dimples at her lumbar, the faint muffin. I massaged her back once after a night in the woods taking mushrooms and sleeping on the tent's bare cover sheet. He stands behind her, draping over her, shout-talking into her ear so she tips her head back. The gloss on her lips I gave to her – applied with a nail-chewed index finger, and she'd said

All right, keep yer clit in yer pants love

The band are retro, garage rock revivalists. Their jeans stop just above their pubic bones. They thunder through their repertoire as if they're falling down the stairs. Oli's other hand touches the small of my back. He mouths close to my ear, so I can feel the heat of his breath but still can't make out most of what he's saying. Something about the band being decent and Mish looking good tonight. Something about going back to his later, in Portslade, and how I can come if I want. His hand on the skin between my strappy top and my unstudded belt.

The band's encore stretches time. Their short shuntalongs replaced by something like a chugging drone that gathers momentum. Six minutes, seven, eight. The singer clutching the mic in both hands, wrapping himself around the stand. He's done with his pose-throwing, his mic-whipping, lassoing. Nine minutes, ten. The lead guitar pushing augmented sevenths, harmonic flashes, power strumming. I play my off-brand Stratocaster in my room, head-phones in, with my bare hands, no pick – play until the fingertips are swollen and red, the hangnails bloody, because it doesn't count if you don't bleed. Oli's arms in the air, Mish's arms in the air, cheering and catcalling with the five-hundred-strong crowd. Mish dreams of travelling the world. Talks of upping and leaving for Mexico when she's done with college, getting some teaching gig in a coastal pueblo. A sea of arms in the air, an ocean of sound.

When the crowd starts spilling out, out into the cool beachside air, steam on the windows, Mish is sleepy drunk. Her left eyelid sitting lower, at an angle. Oli has told me

She's up for it if you are

and

No pressure

The one group of lads I recognise – the year above at college. Wristbeads and skater jeans. The others – who knows. Older, rougher. Maybe they hadn't even been at the gig but chugging cans on the stones outside. The girl with the wristbead boys I recognise too – she was in my Media Studies class for half a term before disappearing. Changed course or dropped out. She was one of those ones who didn't say much, but when she did she spoke like she knew more than everyone else. Voice an octave lower than the other girls' and fried as if by pre-class weed. When the thicknecked one shoves a wristbead so hard he shoots back and tumbleskids through the metal railing sections set-up to show where to queue it's her that gets in the thickneck's face. And in his face she doesn't see, and no-one seems to until it's too late, one of the wristbeads getting cocky, waving a half-empty Sol bottle as if to toss it at the thickneck, and the thickneck's swarthy friend heaving up one section of the railing, as if to swing, and losing balance, and losing his grip, and the railing arcing as he slips.

*

The next evening I'm sitting on the ledge above the promenade, alone, feet dangling. There is no line of gold – cloud cover and traffic, seagull caw.

It begins with me as me, smelling the exhaust fumes from Madeira Drive, rolling a rollie from a pouch of Golden Virginia with Polish health warnings in big mysterious bold font, black on white. I left my MP3 player at Oli's place in Portslade. So I have to play a song in my head instead.

There's nothing in my dreams
but some ugly memories

It begins with me as me, but somewhere in there I'm me as her. I'm me as her getting into Oli's hatchback, me as her rolling on his tobacco-strewn kitchen table, and later, when he's got his wish, I'm me and her at the same time – blurred and blended but with no sense of communion – two ghosts hovering over a scene. After I'd been released from A&E I washed her Minnie Mouse socks by hand, and the water ran rust-red for longer than a song. I meant to give them back but never did.

Kiss me like the ocean breeze

I sing, aloud, in my head, as me, or her, or Iggy Pop, or something in-between, or something else entirely.

Tom Newlands
BEL

Annabel Bray picked up the Binbag nickname about twenty-one years back now. Tony Keown the PE helper took a football team after the school each Thursday, over winter, his own endeavour, up on the blaes, and being good at certain sports like rounders and also being a beanpole, and being really mental quick at running too, Tony softly says to her one wet Wednesday, *really Bel, you should come along.* So she goes and she loves the training, the cones and poles, the regimens, the authentic baltic outdoor feeling, and there's an outfit, a strip – black and dark-gold stripes like a rain-dunked bumble-bee, she thinks, and a badge with the name sewn round: *Cruzie Thistle.* Up on the floodlit pitches by the wastewater plant, after their teas, week on week, a little crew of mouthy local widos come out in the cold to cheer *the Cruzie birds.* And she loves the games at first, too; she runs herself ragged on the crackling blaes and the whole idea of her being a footballer – a *striker* – is kept afloat by everyone's excitement at the speed of her, in the cold. She's see-through-feeling, thin as a hologram, lungs blue, nerves blue, brain blue, skin electric against the itchy strip, legs on fire, running – but running only; never scoring, not like Tony said she would. People gasped real gasps when she ran, everything was right when she ran, but it dawned quite soon (on her at least) that running would be it. But this was Tony's only tactic anyway, his big ploy; the team were to get the ball to her, she was to run towards the goal, and – he never told her where to position herself, how to control the ball, when to pass, how to tackle because, fucked if he knew, he'd never played. He was an *instinct man.* Ice rain, one-nil down to Calderknowes Harriers, eightieth minute, she's sodden, one-on-one with their goalie, Bel shanks it; the ball arcs off toward the corner flag and is smashed through the dark by one of the anoraked local widos, shouting WATCH ME BABE as he thumps it back. It lands in the bushes between the electricity substation and the old brick pavilion: laughter, high-fives, eyes on Bel. Armpit deep in that crisp-packety hedge, bramble-scratched, snotty from rain, a cunt of a wind blasting from somewhere – Edinburgh, probably – she remembers it; the hatred of her own limbs, the tears rimming wobbly and warm, the first aching, emptying, infuriating feeling of letting people you don't care about down. But Tony had already decided discipline was the issue: *you're all effort, you're veering left and right, you're chasing the ball, were you born offside?* She ran more and more but she was waning in the head and she still couldn't score, and the Cruzie didn't ever win. And she fell a lot. And when she fell, in that glittering coral-red grit, it felt like being grated with a grater. And the grazes never healed. And when they didn't heal, they burned. And when they burned she couldn't bolt as quick as everyone needed her to. Savlon never helped. Baths were hell. Soon, and over and over, she tried to quit. Tony smiled his smile, in his gilet, in his River Island brogues, called her his secret weapon, begged her nearly, saying they relied on her speed, that goals will come, please. *Just tell me what to do*, she thought. Nothing improved; Tony's tactic of having a *big rangy lassie* up front had flopped, but he wasn't one for facing up, so he put the blame on her. A blustery Monday half-time, in the changing room, 0–4 down to Braepark Welfare – *fuck sake Annabel think about your positioning, eh, you're blowing about like a fucking binbag in Homebase carpark out there.* Some very small titters from her teammates and a seated glance or two, including from Julie The Goalie, but nothing to suggest an outright rechristening, or that bullying would follow, or that everyone would one day know; in fact, even when the whole team was calling her it it still felt happy and all right and probably temporary. The first sign of something else was in those dismal final weeks, as she sprinted around uncomplainingly, like a circus horse, and the chant went up in mists of breath against the black horizon, from those wee mouthy locals, at her every touch – *Bin-bag, Bin-bag, Bin-bag*; chains in her belly, techno on her tongue, a current of vulnerability blossoming through

her cold frame and rising in prickles to her heart as she blew
aimlessly round the blaes, head lolling like a tulip, shirt a tonne
weight, ears numb, nostrils burning. She could guess how it had
spread out of the changing room, in a *go-on-do-it*, in a *go-on-say-
it-to-her* way, she thought, in huddles and gangs, with eyebrows,
on yellowy-olive Nokia screens; in a way that was designed to hurt.
Tony had stolen it somewhere – the Binbag thing – she knew that
much; he was not a natural and it was too smart a thing to be
coming out his mouth, this guy, this teacher wannabe who had
clearly spent his life working hard to ingratiate himself to people
for whom banter came more easily, and to impress wee kids. He
had the self-certainty of an only child himself, but a slow brain,
and he was not a natural, and even though he wasn't creepy, he
was close; stood there in the changing room, spidery as those
men you saw outside the pool hall, with his crunchy hair-gel hair,
keeping clean, probably mentally cycling through bullet points
he'd memorised from library books about self esteem; grinning,
unnatural as fuck, but trying his best to act the big man, still, in
front of shivery wee lassies in boys boots and shucked-on shirts.
All that didn't matter anyway – they were making a fool of her. But
she had not long to worry about it. A wee nyaff called Leoni McLaren
(Hill High Ladies) went right in on a tackle during the first match
in January, and did Annabel, on purpose. She took a massive
scouring off the wet ground, but there was no pain in the stud-
printed knee as she lay there wheezing on the grit, only hot hot
heat, a sound in her ears like wheels turning, then Leoni McLaren –
who she hardly knew – reappearing, sideways first, then above,
panting over her, blonde hair straggling down with six-p.m. drips,
Big Dipper behind, face red as a house brick, hissing, *Fuck ye Binbag.
Fuck ye, Bel, ya Fenian rat.* Medial collateral ligament tear the
doctor told her, that he normally saw it in boys, that in six-to-eight
weeks she'd be running again, that she was lucky. In the gentle,
sleety afternoons of pain and ballooning after – crutch-bound,
nursing plastic pint cups of microwaved Ribena, her Dad (alive

then) drilling her for info on Leoni McLaren, her big brother going apeshit – she felt only a dark and complicated feeling about that F word; overnight it seemed there was some sort of secret subtext to – to what? To everything? The mood around her as a football player had slipped quickly from amazement to belief to encouragement to faint hope to giggles; was her surname something to do with it? Was being a Fenian the real reason they called her Binbag? Was being a Fenian why the ball never went towards the goal? Being a Fenian seemed to be the reason her knee was now clicking like the lid of a pedal bin when she walked. Was she even Irish though? She didn't know. She wasn't born in Ireland, she'd never set foot there. None of her family had that accent, not even Grandpa Gerald. She was seventeen! It was okay, she thought, to not be too concerned by family trees or the history of the surname Bray; it was okay for a girl at her age to be more interested in Nutella and sicking up gin and books about boys who turned into bats. Even after the six-to-eight weeks, with the crutches in the loft, and her walking again, there was a weird unmendable feeling still, internally, and a gangliness that wasn't there before; an unmanageability about her limbs. Months of thinking eventually had her deciding it was mental, and that she wasn't going back. She flung her boots on the barbecue in spring and her mam tore the strip up for dusters. She hated it when her mind wandered, but at random moments in recent years – putting together her own grown life of coupons and crumbs – maybe on the back step, watching wind steal litter from the sunbleached wheelie bins, or wiping down morning conden- sation with one of her mam's old fake tan towels, or eating chicken balls in bed, she'd remember from nowhere the nickname Binbag. In the queue at the foodbank she'd sometimes see Julie The Goalie, in an own-make coat, with Tippexed nails, and they would nod, say all right, say *howdy*, and Bel would think of herself, for a second or two, holding five tins of marrowfat peas and a pan loaf, as Binbag. At home she would lay on her second-hand sofa and sometimes try and relive the matches, even in momentary highlights, but all she ever managed to bring to life was the before and after; laughing in the ice-air of the brick pavilion changing room, the way that it smelt ahead of the games (fishing tackle and grass and attics) and how it smelt after the games (sweet steam and burny pipes and Pantene). The ecstasy of dragging herself into a silver-hot shower, padding back over the old emulsioned floor, sitting on the wood slat benches boiling, steaming like a ramekin of baked beans, towelling leaf-scraps from her toewebs and forcing her jeans on; the roasty-cheeked gossip as she unhooked and detangled her hoops and lockets from the rusted hooks – that was all good. Then the magic of a quick escape back into the open evening, clean. She remembers hobbling home on the back cycle path for the last time, all centre-parted and talcumed, tasting anti-perspirant aftertaste in the dinnertime dark, and the thought that came that she couldn't stop thinking was that she had fuck all to show for her efforts but a limp, a repositioned kneecap, and that rancid wee nickname Binbag, that, to be fair, did get less rancid as the years went by, and sometimes she even smiled at, because let's face it, she told herself, when alone, some people never do anything nearly memorable enough to earn any sort of nickname. But from that night on, from that wee walk, with the moon a watching saucer and the stars hammered round, something in her teenage-self began to look more cynically on endeavours like sport, and at *joining in*, and at everything really, and, still not sure about what to look forward to in life, she told herself in a woolly way that in future she'd probably want to check she was getting something – money, maybe? – before signing up for things on a whim, before giving away her time and her ligaments and her dignity, not to mention that small piece of brain that seemed to be forever locked into thinking about her own Irishness; about how she never asked her Dad about it, about what she'd ever done to offend Leoni McLaren, about all the words which were clearly scrawled and spoken and texted behind her back, about the conversations which culminated with her lying in the rain with a very hot knee, about that word which had never cropped up before and had never cropped up since but that had undermined her in a way she couldn't understand. And she thought about her Dad; about the height and the flat feet and the knack for solitude he'd given her, how she'd failed to make anything of her gifts. She watches the games now, with the sound off, alone, and feels the movements of the players to be as familiar and foreign to her as the slippery wall of her own disappointed heart – but she would never ever do it again. Bel never liked football, she just wanted to run – moving at speed was natural to her, sprinting felt like self-celebration. She had no real dreams. All she had really wanted was something to get her out of the house on a Thursday night.

Cáit O'Neill McCullagh
FROM THURSO WITH LOVE

In Caithness there's no distinguishing rain from stone as I drive
the coast, half-circling the Cailleach's skirts, her flagstone hems
flat beneath the bosie Beinns – Sutherland, immense with hills

but here, her ankles are tattered by the sea's incessant nipping,
it's a long run in on the north road, the county herself is smaller
still, I'm intent to foot the bar at the corner of Traill & Olrig,

there, open-armed disarming, a kind of Virgil sits shirt-loose
free makking worlds out of such words – *granite, anvil, rune*,
his language was once folded into the great Atlantic, ebbed

firma lifted. Again. Again. Again. The force of it!
I think: *how is it you loose them with such ease*
this rock & ocean? I pick at seams, burst strata

fresh laamer. I'm a stoor-sooker for the words folk speak
poaching their everyday windblow, I neither sort nor sift.
I can feel myself spilling out over your tonsils, he leans to me

loosed words not lost on me. Blushed, I imagine *ochre* & swallow.
Between drams we are drookit with connections – Boru; Clontarf;
Silkbeard; Caithness. We share pities: the turned face of Yeats's da,

the plaintive panes scratched at Croick. In the spaces where we
breathe I hear thunder distant at Dunnet, tune-up *a bag o bunnets*.
Later, tungsten-lit, I see him skip the kerb & he is whistling—

—*From Thurso With Love*

Alistair Paul
FÒGARRAICH

Thuit am fear a-steach dhan tagsaidh aig Ishmael Hussein air a ghualainn air caochan adhar tais, fogharach Glaschu. Bhrag doras an tagsaidh air a chùl a' gearradh dheth gleadhraich na trafaige. Nuair a choimhead Ishmael san sgàthan aige fhuair e sealladh air sgall air a chuairteachadh le nead de dh'fhalt peallach, fliuch. Dh'èirich fàileadh milis, searbh na dibhe às an duine a' lìonadh taobh a-staigh a' chàir. Bha Ishmael air fàs cleachdte ris an fhàileadh sin, ach chan ann aig aon-deug sa mhadainn. Cha do thog an duine a cheann aomte is cha tàinig facal às. Rèitich Ishmael an sat nav air an fhòn na chrochadair ri taobh a' chuibhle stiùiridh is ghearr an seann Nissan Primera aige a-steach dhan dòmhlachadh trafaig mu thimcheall, mar iasg beag is e a' leantainn ri sgaoth mòr. Mar iasg beag shnàmh e a-mach 's a-steach gu clis eadar busaichean is làraidhean. Bha na suathairean air beulaibh Ishmael ag obair gu luaineach a' toirt sealladh priobach dha air glaisead Ghlaschu ceithir timcheall air; glaisead nan togalaichean, glaisead nan daoine is glaisead nan sgothan os a chionn: glaisead a bha fhathast coimheach dha às dèidh dha a bhith a' gabhail còmhnaidh sa bhaile fad ochd mìosan.

Bha e air a dhol seachad air da sheata solais trafaig gun fhacal às a phasaidear mus do leig Ishmael às na faclan, 'Drumgoyne Avenue, a bheil sin ceart?'

Cha tàinig facal às an duine a bha fhathast na shlaod air an t-suidheachan deiridh. Chùm Ishmael air gu ruige an ceann-uidhe a chaidh a shònrachadh dha is e an dòchas, aig a chàr às lugha, nach biodh aige ris an duine a thogail às a' charbad aige an sin no gum biodh aige ri dìobhairt a nighe às na suidheachain aon uair eile. Nam faigheadh e pàigheadh gus nach fhaigheadh b' e sin ceist eile. Bha Ishmael dìreach air tionndadh sìos bho North Frederick Street a-steach gu Cathedral Street nuair a thàinig làmh throm an fhir air a chùl sìos air a ghualann. Chlis Ishmael is thionndaidh e ris an duine. Fo shròin tharraingeadh air falbh an làmh. Thàinig gròcail bhon chùl.

'Duilich, duilich. Cha robh mi airson ur clisgeadh.'

Nuair a choimhead Ishmael san sgàthan a-nis fhuair e sealladh air aogas plumach, glastaidh an duine. Bha cearcaill dhearga mu shùilean. Choinnich na sùilean aige ri clachan beaga, drùidhteach nan sùilean aig an duine. Choimhead e an dàrna taobh.

''S e dìreach nach eil sin ceart,' thuirt an duine. Bha na faclan aige nas coileanta na bha Ishmael an dùil is thàinig e a-steach air gur dòcha gun robh rudeigin a bharrachd air an deoch a' cur air.

'Dè?'

'Drumgoyne Avenue. Chan eil sin ceart.'

''S e sin a th' agam. Sin far a bheil sinn a' dol.'

'Cha tèid agam air a dhol an sin.'

Ghearr an Nissan aig Ishmael gu cruinn seachad air bus a dh'fhiar a-steach air a bheulaibh gu stad. Shàth e a' chas air a' bhrèig is an làraidh, a bha na stad an sin gus tionndadh far an rathad mhòr, a' tighinn gu h-obann san t-sealladh dha. Cha robh e an gnè Ishmael a bhith mì-mhodhail ach bha an suidheachadh san robh e ga chur droil. Thionndaidh e ris an duine air a chùl.

'Feumaidh mi an t-slighe a chaidh a thoirt dhomh a leantainn,' spliathartaich e le mì-fhoighidinn na ghuth.

Gun fhreagairt às an duine air a chùl chùm Ishmael a' dol. Bha e air a dhol fon M8 is e a' gearradh sìos Hawthorn Street eadar teanamantan ruadha is feansa àrd ionad ghnìomhachais Cowlairs nuair a thàinig lasgan bhon chùl.

'Inbhir Nis!'

'B' àill leibh?'

'Inbhir Nis!'

'Inbhir dè?'

'Inbhir Nis, siud far an tèid mi. Siud an aon àite dhan tèid mi.'

Thoinn na làmhan aig Ishmael gu frionasach air a' chuibhle stiùiridh.

Sràid Inbhir Nis? Avenue Inbhir Nis?

Le corragan a dhàrna làimh bha Ishmael a' strì ris an ainm choimheach a chur a-steach dhan ap sat nav aige is an làmh eile aige greimichte ris a' chuibhle.

'Baile Inbhir Nis.'

Le sin ghearr Ishmael far an rathad air cùl bhana Hermes a bha na stad an sin. Aig oir a shùla rèitich an t-slighe air a' fòn aige. Thàinig gròcail ghrànda às a' bhrèig làimh is Ishmael a' tarraing air gu teann. Thionndaidh e ris an duine air a chùl.

'Tha sin ceud, ceithir fichead sa h-ochd puing a còig mìltean air falbh bho seo.'

Gun fhios aige dè bu chòir dha dhèanamh dh'fhòn Ishmael a-steach dhan ionad stiùiridh aige. Dh'èirich torman ghuthan sradagach fad tamaill bhon toiseach. Thionndaidh e ris a' phasaidear aige às ùr.

'Thèid agam air sin a dhèanamh, ach feumaidh sibh pàigheadh an toiseach.'

Rùraich an duine gu cearbach na phòcaid bhroillich. An ceann ùine a-mach às doimhneachd seacaid lorcach, mhì-sgiobalta an duine dh'èirich màileid-phòca shnasach, sgiobalta. Thilg an duine fosgailte i air a shliasaid a' toirt am follais sreath de chairtean creideis is trusan tiugh de nòtaichean air am filleadh gu cuimir a-steach dhan phòcaid air an cùlaibh. A rèir fianais a sporain cha b' e seo fear a bha gann de stòras. Tharraing Ishmael an t-inneal chairt-chreideis aige a-mach às an t-seotal fon deas-bhòrd is air dha na fiogairean ceart a bhruthadh a-steach ann thabhainn e air an duine, a bha a' strì ri cairt fhaighinn às a' mhàileid-phòca aige, e.

'An urrainn dhomh?' Thuirt Ishmael is le aon ghluasad ealamh spìon e a' chairt a-mach is smèid e thar an inneil i. Phut e a' chairt air ais dhan mhàileid-phòca is le aon ghlùin air an t-seithir aige is e a' crochadh a-steach dhan chùl chuir e a' mhàileid-phòca air ais ann am pòcaid an duine.

Chunnacas iasg beag gorm an Nissan aig Ishmael a' snàmh bho seo tro alltan is leas-aibhnichean Springburn, seachad air iomall

Roinn Goilf Littleton agus Pàirc Robroyston agus a-nìos gu abhainn mhòr an M8. Mun àm a dh'fhiar e a-steach dhan t-sruth air cùl bus City Link bha am pasaidear aige na shuain cadal sa chùl is e a' srann gu plathach. Ged a bha an càr aig Ishmael na iasg clis am measg trafaig a' bhaile, a' gearradh a-mach 's a-steach gu dàna eadar sreathan, an seo bha e taobh a-muigh àrainneachd dualaiche is e a' gluasad gu mall, cùramach le làraidhean is fiù 's carabhanaichean a' dol seachad air. On a ràinig e Glaschu cha robh Ishmael a-riamh air a bhith taobh a-muigh crìochan a' bhaile. Nuair a bha e air sruthadh air falbh bhon M8 a-mach air an M80 is an rathad air socrachadh beagan chuir e làmh a-steach gu pòcaid a bhriogais is thug e a-mach da dhealbh a chàraich e air an t-seithir ri thaobh. Thug e plathadh sìos orra is choimhead na trì rudan as prìseile dha san t-saoghal suas airsan. Sin a bhean ann an aon de na deilbh air latha am pòsaidh is na mìog-sùilean cruinn, donn aice a' coimhead suas air; beannag phurpaidh òr ghrinn mu a ceann is pàtaran toinnte henna air na làmhan sìnte roimhpe. Gach turas a laigheadh a shùil air an dealbh thigeadh an là sin air ais thuige mar gur ann an dè a bh' ann; na mnathan a' crònan is a' gusgal is poitean an fheusta air an cinn, fàileadh a' bhìdh, na fir sna ròban geala air an cruinneachadh fon t-seann chraoibh Acacia aig meadhan a' bhaile, a' chlann ri cleasachd is spòrs ag itealaich nan sgaothan mu na h-inbhich. A h-uile rud cho soilleir, dathach. Ri taobh, san dealbh eile, an dà nighean aig Ishmael, is measgachadh de chleasachd is bàidh ri fhaicinn sna sùilean acasan. Gach turas a laigheadh a shùilean air an dealbh sin a-nis 's i a' cheist a thigeadh thuige; 'Saoil dè an coltas a bhiodh orra a-nis?'; is bliadhna air a dhol seachad bhon là a thàinig air soraidh fhàgail aca. B' iad na h-ìomhaighean sin an acair aig Ishmael, greimichte leis a' ghrunnd, a' cur stad air bho bhith a falbh leis an t-sruth. B' iad sin a thug dha adhbhar a chumail a' dol is dòchas aige, aon uair 's gun rachadh aige air an obair phàipeir a choileanadh is beagan airgid a chur mu seach, gun tigeadh iad còmhla a-rithist.

Bha an tagsaidh aig Ishmael air a dhol seachad air Peairt is a'
dlùthadh ri Baile Chloichridh mus do dhùisg am pasaidear aige
le cnead. Shuidh an duine an àrd le clisgeadh.

'Feumaidh sinn stad,' ghrad-ghlaodh e.

Choimhead Ishmael mu thimcheall. Air oir an rathaid bha crash
barrier is eadar sin is an tarmac cha robh ann ach stiall thana feòir.

'Chan urrainn dhomh!'

'An sin!' chomharraich an duine claon-rathad air am beulaibh.

Shlug an rathad sin an tagsaidh aig Ishmael sìos sgòrnan lùbach
tarmac eadar craobhan àrda ga fhàgail air rathad dìreach a ruith
an co-shìneadh ris an Uisge Teimheil. Ghearr Ishmael a-steach an
sin dhan chiad àite pàircidh a chunnaic e. Cha robh an càr aige
fiù 's air tighinn buileach gu stad na bha an duine a-mach air an
doras is seachad air a' ghàrradh ri taobh an rathaid le cruinn-leum.
Ged nach fhaiceadh Ishmael ach ceann an duine is cùl aige
ris chluinneadh e an steall farmadach a thàinig às is e a' taomadh
le neart air an fheur aig a chasan. Thog Ishmael an dà dhealbh
bhon t-seithir a dhinn e gu h-ealamh air ais dhan phòcaid aige is
choimhead e an dàrna taobh. Dh'fheith e . . . Agus dh'fheith e. Mu
dheireadh thall thug e sùil air ais gu far am bu chòir dhan phasaidear
aige a bhith ach cha robh sgeul air. Shlaighd Ishmael e fhèin thairis
air suidheachan a' phasaideir ri thaobh gus nach nochdadh e air
beulaibh trafaig an rathaid is dh'fhalbh e an càr. Thug esan grad
leum a-nis thairis air a' ghàrradh ach cha d' fhuair e an sin ach
bruach fheurach shleamhainn is bras sruth na h-aibhne an sin foidhe,
gun sgeul air an duine. Cha tug e fada 's e na sheasamh an sin na
thuaineal gus an do dh'fhairich e an t-uisge fuar a' drùthadh a-steach
dhan trainers tana aige bhon talamh bhog fodhpa. Tro throman
socair an uisge chluinneadh e cneadail. Thionndaidh e agus sin
am pasaidear aige na shlaod ris a' ghàrradh is e a' gal mar leanabh.
Chliob Ishmael air ais suas a' bhruach gu far an robh an duine.

''S còir dhuinn cumail oirnn,' thuirt e. Le sin chuir e làimh fo
achlais an duine ga chuideachadh gu a chois is an uair sin thairis

air a' ghàrradh. Thuit an dithis a-steach dhan chàr is lean iad
orra tro Bhaile Chloichridh is air ais suas dhan A9. Bha casan
Ishmael a-nis bog fluich. Chuir e air siostam teasachaidh a' chàir
aig àirde an oidhirp an tioramachadh, a' cur trùman a' ghaotharain
ri burral an einnsein is grunnsgal nan lòraidhean san dol seachad
orra. Tron fharam thàinig guth an duine sa chùl.

'Do-sheachanta saoilidh mi. Mar a thachair. 'S fhada on a tha
cùisean air a bhith a' dol leis a' bhruthach.' Le teanga air fhuasgladh
thàinig na faclan nan steall a-nis, dìreach mar a thàinig am muin
na bu thràithe, is na briathran a bha air a bhith ag ad na bhroinn
mar ball teinne ag ad ann an bholcàno, ga losgadh air an taobh
a-staigh, a' spreidheadh às. Sna beagan mìltean a lean fhuair Ishmael
làn a sheanchais. Mun chonas nimheil a bha air a bhith ann an
oidhche a-raoir eadar esan is a bhean. An esan a choisich a-mach
no an ise a thilg a-mach e cha robh e soilleir ach fhuair e e fhèin
ann an taigh charaid is bha iad air teannadh ri òl. A-mach an
uairsin leotha gu taigh-seinnse is an uair sin gu club-oidhche.
Dh'fhàs cùisean doilleir aig an ìresa ach bha cuimhne mhath aige
air na leotards bhian-liopaird a bha air buill a' phartaidh chirce
san deach iad an sàs. Ann an uairean beaga na maidne bha a charaid
air falbh le tè de na boireannaich ga fhàgail na aonar. Bha e air
dùsgadh air beinge ann an Stèisean Thrèanaichean Sràide na
Bànrighinn.

Às dèidh dha leumadh a-steach dhan tagsaidh thàinig air ais
thuige na rudan suarach a chaidh a ràdh aig àird an tabaid an
oidhche a-raoir. Cha robh dòigh a b' urrainn dha dìreach nochdadh
air ais air an stairsich is gach tàthag is cronachadh is casaid a chaidh
èigheachd fhathast na chrochadh os a cionn. B' e Inbhir Nis àite
àraich is màthair is bràthair dha fhathast a' fuireach ann. Bha e air
faighinn a-mach cho beag feum 's a bha caraidean nuair a bha feum
aige orra. Aig deireadh gnothaich 's e dàimh teaghlaich an aon
dàimh as fhiach.

Bha sgoltaidhean air nochdadh sa chòmhdach thiugh de sgothan
os an cionn is colbhan solais a' briseadh tromhpa a' soilleireachadh

ruadh-donn fogharail nan slèibhtean aig astar is a' cur lainnir air
na h-altan a mhir troimhe. Sna beanntan àrda aig cùl an t-seallaidh
bha brèidean sneachda air an crochadh an siud 's an seo am falachan
nan coirean.

'Tha an dùthaich agaibh àlainn.' Thuirt Ishmael. 'Cha robh fhios
agam gun robh i cho bòidheach.'

Tharraing na faclan aig Ishmael an duine às breislich a smuaintean
tamall, is choimhead e mu thimcheall air.

'Tha. Tha sibh ceart.'

Lìon còisir meacanaigeach às ùr an clos a lean sa chòmhradh,
clos a thug an dithis thairis air Druim Uachdair is a-steach am
measg crainn ghiuthais is raointean farsaing Srath Spè. Bha am
Monadh Ruadh air faire is an Nissan aig Ishmael a' gearradh eadar
tobhta Taigh Feachd Ruadhainn na seasamh air a' chnoc chruinn
dhan dàrna taobh is Baile Ceann a' Ghiuthsaich na shìneadh fodhpa
air an taobh eile mus do chuir an duine crìoch air a sheanchas.

'Thèid agam air a bhith beò às a h-aonais. Bidh e duilich 's
cinnteach ach nì mi an gnothach air, mu dheireadh thall. Ach 's e
mo mhac, cha tèid agam air a bhith dealaichte bhon rud as prìseil
dhomh san t-saoghal air fad.'

Clos a-rithist a thug iad seachad air an Aghaidh Mhòr is a-nìos
gu ruige an slochd mus do bhruidhinn an duine a rithist.

'Dè dhèanadh tusa? Duilich, chan eil fhios agam dè an t-ainm a
tha ort?'

'Ishmael.'

'Ishmael, dè dhèanadh tusa?'

Mheòraich Ishmael air a' cheist fad ùine mhòir mus tug e seachad
a fhreagairt.

''S chòir dhuibh "duilich" a ràdh rithe. Mathanas iarraidh oirre.'

Shuidh am pasaidear an àrd is dhlùthaich e air Ishmael gus
an do dh'fhairich Ishmael anail air cùl amhaich. 'Chan urrainn
dhomh sin a dhèanamh. Cha do rinn mi dad a bha ceàrr. Chan
eil aithreachas orm mu aon fhacal a thuirt mi. An fhirinn a
th' agam.'

'Chan eil e gu diofar cò às coireach. Cha chosg am facal "duilich" sgillinn dhuibh. 'S còir dhuibh "duilich" a ràdh.'

Thuit an duine air ais san t-suidheachan aige gun smid às. An ceann ùine dh'èirich cruth Inbhir Nis bhon tarmac air beulaibh Ishmael is an Nissan a' cromadh an rathad roinnte dha ionnsaigh le Linne Mhoireabh is Drochaid Ceasaig air a chùl. Thug Ishmael sùil fhiar air an t-sat nav. Ghrad amhairc e san sgathan. 'Tha sinn gus Inbhir Nis; an e sin ainm an àite? Tha sinn gus Inbhir Nis a ruighinn. A bheil seòladh agaibh? Cait an tèid sinn a-nis?' Thug e sùil chlis eile air an t-sat nav. 'Tha sinn a' dlùthadh ri cearcall-rathaid.'

Phriob togalaichean Inbhir Nis orra bho air cùl nan craobhan rin taobh is an cearcall-rathaid a' sìor dhèanamh orra. Dh'fheith am pasaidear gus an robh iad air an slighe a-steach dhan chearcall greimichte eadar dà lòraidh tomadach mus tug e seachad a fhreagairt.

'Rach timcheall an cearcall-rathaid is tillidh sinn a Ghlaschu.'

Andy Raffan
LIGHTS IN THE DARKNESS

Three minutes to ten on a Friday night and fucking stuck in here again! Tommy glared at the clock, pushed his glasses back and brushed away the fringe of dark hair from his forehead. This summer job clung to him like seaweed on rocks. Sighing, he continued mopping the yellow plastic floor in a way that rearranged the tramped-in muck rather than cleaned it. He was almost back at the counter, the till and lottery machine framed by a garish display of alcohol bottles cheered on by a chorus line of cigarettes. Above them in lurid green letters ran the company slogan – *At the Heart of the Community*. Aye right, he thought, only if that community was having a fucking heart attack at the prices.

'C'mon, let's start cashing up,' said Jean, bustling through the storeroom door and tossing her cigarettes onto the counter. Her face wore its perpetual look of disappointment. 'I dinna want to hang around any later than I huv tae.'

Tommy jammed the filthy mop into the half empty bucket. 'Eh, aye . . . okay, if you say so,' he replied and tip-toed across the wet floor to the door. He turned the sign to Closed and snapped the lock shut. Then he navigated his way back and began emptying the till and passing the notes to Jean. He looked down at her tied-back greying hair, her small hands deftly sorting. She emanated a mixture of stale smoke and wet dog.

'What's this?' he said, peeling two twenties apart. Stuck between was a grubby piece of folded notepaper. He opened it.

Jean turned. 'C'mon, hurry up. Chuck that in the bin.'

'Wait. Hold on.' His face paled and he leaned back against the counter. 'Bloody hell, check this.' He passed the note over. Jean's eyes scanned down, then she gave out a snort.

'Ach, someone's winding us up.'

'What if it's real? What if someone's gonnae . . .'

'Kill themselves? And leave their suicide note here?'

Tommy straightened up. 'We've got to do something. We cannae just let it happen again!'

Jean stared at him, then her expression softened. 'That was an accident, Tommy. You know there's nothing you could have done.'

'Give me it.' He snatched the paper out of her hand. 'Look,' he said, pointing, 'it's signed. I mind now. Old Ian, he was in earlier. He gave me two twenties.'

'That old alky? I've no seen him in ages.' Jean tutted and folded her arms. 'They're all the same. Dinna care about anyone but themselves. And God knows the last thing they want is someone trying tae help.'

'I know where he lives, I've taken deliveries oot.' Tommy grabbed his coat and ran toward the door.

'Ye canna leave me alone with all this cash. If you go don't bother coming back the morrow.'

Tommy turned sharply, almost slipping. 'You know I have to go,' he said. Jean stood with her arms wrapped tight across her chest. Then she sighed and nodded. Tommy turned, unlocked the door, and disappeared into the darkness.

*

He ran through the High Street, long coat flapping like wings, breath misting. He passed The Bothy. Shouts and music spilled out, a comfort blanket smothering the huddled smokers outside.

'Left the gas on eh Tommy?' shouted one and they laughed; too loud, the alcohol firing them like petrol on flames. He ran on, ignoring them. But he'd known a few of the faces. Same age as Paul. Still death-spiralling in the same Friday night dance.

Now he could see the orange lights from the harbour. A few small boats motionless on the flat dark water. The grey concrete wall like a crooked arm sheltering them as a schoolchild hides their jotter from prying classmates. His stomach turned and he focused on the quiet street ahead.

They'd moved here ten years earlier. Dad had gone by then and Mum wanted to be closer to family. The day they arrived she'd chased him and his older brother Paul out from the cramped cottage. Walking round the village Paul was moody at the smallness of the place. They'd ended up at the seafront as a storm was building, great grey artillery shells of clouds scudding across the sky. Angry looking waves were rolling up, slamming into the back wall of the harbour then shooting upwards like long white finger bones before falling and soaking the inner walkway. Paul had run to the end where the waves were hitting, Tommy trailing behind uncertain. Once there they'd clung to the freezing railings and screamed as the icy waves lifted into the air then dropped down to soak them. Tommy had shouted his hands were slipping and Paul had turned and taken a fierce grip of his coat until a break in the waves let them race back along the harbour.

When they'd eventually squelched home their mother had yelled at Paul for what seemed like hours. Neither was allowed out again for a week. Afterwards his brother seemed to be constantly telling him what to do. Yet almost in the same breath Paul was fighting with the village kids who shouted 'four eyes' and 'teacher's pet' at Tommy. Something had changed but he wasn't sure what.

*

He was at the end of the village now. Beyond lay the dark outline of the headland and the white zigzags of the waves. His chest burned from freezing gulps of air, and he slowed, examining the row of former fishermen's cottages. That one, the one with the rusty anchor propped against the outside wall. No light came through the small windows. He walked up to the door and rattled the letterbox. No sound from inside. He rattled it again, knocking this time as well. Nothing. He paused. Then he turned the handle and pushed. Locked.

'Shit!' he said. Then he remembered. Deliveries got dropped off at the back door. It was the kind of place where back doors were never locked, and front doors only opened for the minister, or the arrival of a long-lost relative returned from overseas. He ran round the windowless gable end with its large uneven bricks softened by the wind whipping off the Firth.

'Who's that?' A figure stood outlined against the sky at the edge of the garden. Tommy opened the gate and walked over. Ian stood next to two metal framed deck chairs that faced seaward, the striped fabric just muted greys in the dark. He was wearing a heavy coat and a dark woolly hat. What little light there was glinted from the binoculars hanging round his neck.

'It's me. Tommy,' he gasped, 'You know, from the shop.'

'Bit late for deliveries eh son?'

'Aye, I suppose. I was just passing and,' he paused, 'I thought I heard a noise. Like burglars . . . or something.'

'Good thing I've nothin' worth stealing then eh?' said Ian, laughing. 'Sounds like you need to catch your breath. Sit doon.' He settled into the nearest chair.

Tommy looked at him then sat in the other chair. It creaked as if pondering a collapse. He looked out at the sky. There was no moon, and the streetlights didn't stretch this far. As his eyes adjusted stars began to appear in the black gaps the way heated popcorn fills a pot.

'Are you all right?' said Tommy.

'I was watching for meteorites.'

'Meteorites?'

'Shooting stars, ye ken. This is the first time since . . . well, it's the first clear night in a long time.' The old man turned. 'Shouldn't you be away to the college by now?'

Tommy looked away. He thought of the brown envelopes sitting unopened in the drawer next to his bed.

'We saw the Northern Lights once,' said Tommy. 'I must have been nine or ten. I remember the sky was all green and purple. And it crackled too.'

They'd hung out their bedroom window, Paul's face next to his, the glow of the aurora reflecting in his eyes like the innards of the marbles in the jar between their beds. Paul had whispered how it was particles from the sun hitting the atmosphere and he'd pictured them as yellow tentacles stretching out from the sun to grab the Earth and bathe it in soft flames.

'Youse were lucky. It's a rare thing that,' said Ian. 'Meteorites are more predictable.'

Out of the corner of his eye Tommy saw a flash of light arc across the sky. He jumped up, pointing out to sea. 'Was that one?' he shouted.

'Aye, it was. That's the start of the Orionids. Rita told me all about them. She was the one who knew all about the astronomy.'

Tommy watched the sky. Then he reached into his pocket. 'Mr Sutherland, I found this note in the shop. I read it and . . . well . . .' He sat down and held it out, his hand shaking. The older man took it and produced a small torch. He looked at it silently for a minute. Then he looked at Tommy and handed the note back.

'I was in a bad way for a bit. Y'know. Afterwards. Sometimes you feel like there's no point.' Tommy nodded.

'I wrote that a while back. But I couldnae do it. I minded how she told me there's a whole universe out there if you look hard enough. I felt I still had a wee bit more to see yet.'

Tommy thought back to that night in April. Paul had come home late. He'd stood in the middle of their bedroom. This time though he wasn't swaying, and his words were clear, not slurred.

'Tom,' he'd whispered, 'dinna listen tae them fuckers. You've got the golden ticket oot o this place. So take it, and dinna look back. And once ye're gone, forget aboot us.'

'Shut up, how can I? You'll be coming doon at weekends to drink in aw they pubs wi me and pullin they student girls.'

Paul had laughed, low and quiet. 'Naw. We're all just holding ye back. I'm just holding ye back. Ah'm trapped here. But you, you've got the chance. Take it and run as far as ye can.' Then he'd gone downstairs. Tommy had listened for him coming back up but had fallen asleep waiting.

They found Paul the next morning floating in the flat dark water of the harbour. A sparse crowd had gathered at the waterside, smoking, talking in low voices while they waited for the police to arrive from Inverness. Death by misadventure the inquest would say. Too much drink. Slipped and hit his head on one of the boats. Case closed.

Tommy knew different. And as he'd stood by the graveside with glassy shards of sleet on his face and the cord slipping rough through his tenuous hands, he'd looked at his mother, small and broken, and she'd looked back at him, and he could tell she knew different too.

*

The old man sniffed. 'Can ye imagine how long those rocks have been oot there before shootin across the sky? Tiny wee things too, but when they hit the atmosphere – whoosh, a flash of life then gone.'

'How long does it go on for?' said Tommy.

'Och, a few hours if ye're lucky. Ye know, every time I see one it reminds me of her. In a good way.'

'Would it be all right if I stayed to watch them with you?'

'Aye, sure.' The older man was quiet for a moment. 'You watchin for anyone in particular?'

'Just for someone who couldnae make it this far,' replied Tommy, and in his pocket he crumpled an old piece of paper and gazed into the sky, waiting for a light in the darkness.

Martin Raymond
MESSENGERS AT ARMS

Doorsteps. It was where they spent their days, waiting.

'She's coming this time,' said Old Callum, 'I can feel it in my bones.' He was a few paces back from the porch. It didn't do to be standing like a small crowd, best give the customer some room. Behind Old Callum was the glazed lawn, the drive with the Range Rover, heavy and smug on the mono-block drive. Beyond were white hills and the sharp colours of the Moray Firth. This was Old Callum's last day, and Calum tried to fix this image in his head, his colleague of eight years, set against the landscape.

The door opened and a woman's face appeared in the gap, blonde hair and hostile eyes.

'Mrs Coldwater?' said Calum.

'Not today, thank you.' The door closed. Calum sighed and pressed the bell again.

This time the door was yanked all the way open. The woman was dressed in a velour top and patterned leggings that could have been part of an eye test. There was a smell of perfume and new carpet.

'What.'

'Good morning. Mrs Elaine Coldwater?'

'Yes.'

'You are the registered keeper of vehicle registration TH55 MUM?'

'So?'

'I am Calum Naismith, and this is my colleague Callum Macleod, we are from Glen and Glen Sheriff Officers. We have a court order on behalf of Tulloch Motor Factors to . . .'

The door slammed shut. He turned to look at Old Callum who nodded with appreciation. They were connoisseurs of the aggressively handled door. This one, although attached to a new-build, had an admirable heft to it. Old Callum leant into the porch and stroked the varnished wood.

'Nice,' he said, as Calum pressed the bell again. Patience was their virtue. Across the road a neighbour was salting her driveway with great care.

Suddenly the door was open again. Mrs Coldwater leant against the doorway. Was the zip on the velour top slightly further down than before? It wouldn't be the first time, and it was one of the reasons why Old Callum was here as a witness.

'I've spoken to my husband.' She smiled. 'It's just a bit of confusion, crossed wires. There is no problem.'

Calum had heard the crossed wires thing before. And about the absence of any problem.

'I'm sorry, it's not for me to debate this with you. You have to pass me the keys and documents and . . .'

Another slam. After a while the keys were shoved at them through the letterbox. Calum picked them off the inlaid mat. He got into the Range Rover and adjusted the seats and mirror. The neighbour had given up with the salting; now she was pecking her mobile with long turquoise nails. Why didn't they just hand over the keys, get it over with without fuss? He and Old Callum used to joke that it was like the stages of grief; denial, anger, all the way to acceptance. But then Old Callum's wife died of cancer and it wasn't so funny.

Tullochs were delighted to see their car again, but Calum understood how most people viewed his job. There was often mockery or resentment, tales of how dim or officious or cruel the men on the doorstep could be, and always wariness, a distance. They didn't understand that he was a vital part of a system that kept money flowing and lots of people in a job.

Apart from Old Callum, who wouldn't be coming back in on Monday.

'You'll have plenty to do though, with your time?' Calum was driving. They were out of town now, heading north and west. After dropping off the re-possession they had worked through their list – serving papers, making final, final demands and listening to tales of desperation, dispatches from the end of the line.

'Och yes, I'm sure I'll get the gist of it,' said Old Callum. He was staring straight ahead, the bleak winter hills to the left. 'I'm at an age to have my feet up and not be out here in the cold, chasing my tail.'

'Don't you go that funny way they go. You retired people with your puzzle-books and your writing to complain about everything.'

'That's my plan,' said Old Callum, '"To Whom it May Concern, it has come to my attention that the laburnum hedge at 53 Braemar Way is an affront to decent public morals."'

Calum stopped at road works. Heather misted way into the distance, the hills beginning to blur as the hard, frosty start dissolved into drizzle.

'But don't you worry, you'll have Willie's chat to entertain you.'

Willie was in the back foot-well, folded neatly. A tabard with discreet reflective piping and a body worn camera, it had replaced Old Callum. From now on the officers could travel alone. They called it Willie the Witless Witness. Everyone would behave better if they were being filmed, it was said. They'd been consulted and ignored, so that was that.

'It will be interesting to see how Willie takes to the dogs.'

'The dogs,' said Old Callum, 'the dogs will take a bit of practice, there's nothing surer.' Old Callum's way with dangerous dogs was legendary. They were off the main roads now, a single track with few passing places, the sat nav suddenly quiet, humbled.

'That'll be us,' said Calum. 'Your last job.'

It was a compact cottage, still the property of the estate and so lacking any improvements. They left the car by the roadside and crossed the feral lawn. Calum stepped over the submerged rusty frame of a child's bike. There was a chainless chainsaw by a derelict shed.

Another door, the green paint blistered. Calum knocked and after a while it opened, scrapping on the cement floor. The woman was tiny, her eyes borrowed from someone much bigger. She was maybe in her late twenties, and she was carrying a baby. The

landowner wanted the cottage empty, to be spruced up in time for
the season. The occupant was seven months in arrears, all due
process had been followed, all warnings given.

'Mrs . . .?' said Calum.

'Miss Teviot.'

'Is Mr Petrauskas at home?' Calum asked, although he knew
the answer.

'He's away. Working.'

As Calum explained the Court Order it was clear that all of this
was news to her.

'But Arnas sorted all this out.'

'This is why we're here,' said Calum, 'because he didn't sort
it out.'

She stood square in the doorway.

'May we come in? Arrangements. You need to get sorted out,
what with him . . .' He reached for the baby's hand. She pulled
the child out of reach.

'It's her. You'd better come in.'

There were two climates inside, the hallway as cold as the glen
outside and the living room nearly tropical. The woman's feet were
bare, her toenails a chipped scarlet. A neat pile of identical brown
envelopes on the mantelpiece above the fire were unopened. They
were from Highland Health Board, not Calum's firm.

'Is there anyone you can stay with in the short term. Tonight, I
mean?' Calum didn't do as many evictions as people thought. They
weren't like recovering a 4x4.

'But Arnas sorted this out. I can phone him now, you can speak
to him.'

The mother put the baby into the car seat on the floor. It was so
quiet – only the gurgling of the baby and an occasional spark from
the fire – that they could all listen as the phone rang out for a long
time, then stopped.

She put the phone down on the table next to a large, curved dent
in the fake wood.

'We understand that Mr Petrauskas has gone back to Vilnius,' said Calum, 'to the family home.'

As soon as he said the words he saw her face change, it was the moment when you stub your toe in the dark, just before the pain.

'But that's not where he is. He's working in Newcastle. He'll be back at the end of the month. That's why he paid the rent until then.'

'There's been no rent paid since . . .'

'And anyway he's not got any family in Vilnius, his mother's in London and his father is dead.'

Calum had been to Vilnius. It had been his brother's stag weekend, he and five of his brother's pals. He thought of the miles of identical apartments out to the airport, hazy through the hangover. He imagined Mr Petrauskas with earphones on in one of those flats, another baby asleep in the corner, a blonde woman opening a door, dressed for work in her business suit. They had all been blonde, so classy and smart that he'd thought they should be dressed in suits or white lab coats rather than heels and body glitter. The oral sex had cost less than a round of drinks, which even at the time felt wrong.

'We need to get you sorted though. Somewhere to stay. Do you have enough cash?' She shrugged and pointed vaguely towards nothing in particular.

'We can get you to Inverness. There really isn't any choice, the landlord wants to re-possess at noon.' She didn't seem to be listening, her fingers polishing the black screen of the phone.

'Why did you say family home when there isn't one? Just then.'

He considered all the options, but experience taught him it was best not to lie. 'Because that's what we've been told, he's with his family. Your name's not on any documents so we won't pursue you for arrears.'

But she wasn't interested now. Her toes curled on the thin carpet. Old Callum was entertaining the baby, appearing and disappearing from behind the edge of the blanket.

'Are you okay?' Old Callum spoke from the floor. 'Can we make you tea or something? Help you get ready?'

She had got away from them now, looking out the small window at the wet hillside.

'When?'

'The landlord wants the place back within the hour; he's given you months of notice.'

She tapped her phone. It lit up and she was there, windswept, with a dark-haired man and the baby wrapped in a one-piece suit.

'Give us till two. Please.'

'I'll keep the landlord informed, but you must go before two,' said Calum. 'We'll be back on the nail.'

They drove back down the glen to a lochan.

'Poor lassie,' said Calum.

'Bastard men,' said Old Callum. 'Always the same.'

'"Oh, by the way, did I mention the family I have previously? It's not a problem if I just go back to my former life is it?"'

'Exactly that. Bonnie bairn, too.'

'At least we'll let her go in her own time.'

The lochan was almost black and clouds cut the hills off mid-slope. Calum phoned the client in London.

'God's sake!' The voice boomed at them. 'I'm not sure what I'm paying you people for. Two o'clock is not what I agreed. I've got tradesmen waiting.'

He rang off. Calum checked the call was finished.

'You'll be in trouble,' said Old Callum.

'Don't care. You have to cut some slack.'

They looked out over the lochan. At the far side two swans were so white against the dark water they looked as if they were illuminated from inside. Old Callum unfolded his sandwiches, the precise foil parcel.

'Just think, from now on you can come out to places like this any time you like.'

They both thought about that for a while as the wind buffeted the car.

'Vilnius, eh? You had a time there, I mind you telling me. Do you see your brother much? Nottingham he lives now, isn't it?'

'Leicester. No, only now and again. He's busy, too.'

They were quiet for a while in the wind. Above their cups on the dashboard identical flares of condensation crept up the windscreen and died back.

'Ah well,' said Old Callum, 'I must venture out. It's the cold weather.'

'Nonsense,' said Calum, 'it's your auld bladder, like a deflated balloon by now. But I'll join you to be on the safe side.'

They stood together as the wind rippled the loch. The swans had gone but neither had seen them take off.

At the cottage Calum checked the car clock – 14:00. There was no answer to his knocks. The door was unlocked, but when Calum pushed, something heavy stopped it opening. The curtains weren't drawn all the way. They both peered through the gap. The baby was strapped into the carrying seat, a blanket tucked in all round and a knitted hat on her head. Beside her there was a large plastic baby-bag with a smiling pink elephant on the side. The fire was dying back behind a heavy iron guard.

'Keek the letter box,' said Old Callum, 'she's maybe still packing upstairs.'

Chapping the doors, keeking the boxes – Calum's future stretched away.

He pushed the flap. What he saw were ten toes, all with fresh, flawless scarlet nail-polish. His instinct was to shoulder the door, but he couldn't bring himself to shove her out of the way, so he followed Old Callum round the back where the kitchen door was open, ready for them. They found a kitchen knife to cut down the sheet. Neither of them could look at her face as they struggled with the knot.

The baby only woke later when the police arrived, before the ambulance and the social worker.

'I don't know how you boys do things,' the sergeant had said, when they were walking back to the cars, 'but there's numbers people like us can call, after a thing like this.'

They drove back to the main roads, and when silence stopped being helpful Calum said,

'Some last day.'

'Yes,' said Old Callum. 'Touch and go. But she'll be okay.'

'Probably, but that was quite the cry for help.'

They had the headlights on now, the rain streaking under the wipers. Calum wondered how her day would have been if the cottage hadn't been on their list, if he hadn't mentioned the family. If they'd spent longer at the lochan.

'It's never the money,' said Old Callum. 'It's always love. Nothing we can do about that.'

'True,' said Calum, concentrating on the road. It was a while before he realised how hard he was gripping the wheel.

By the time they got to their office, the building was in darkness and the street almost empty of cars. Calum thought about Old Callum going home to his dark bungalow. Calum always left his own hall light on through the winter – to deter intruders. Or so he told himself. They'd never socialised, the two Callums. They said that's why they were such a good team.

He pulled up behind Old Callum's small hatchback. Lit up by the white street lights, a squall of rain came down the street. It lashed the car.

'There's a bottle of malt in there for you.' Calum nodded towards the dark office.

'I'll maybe get it later.'

They sat watching water run down the windscreen.

'Are you busy Saturday?' said Calum.

'I'm through in Aberdeen,' he said. 'Sister's.'

'Course,' said Calum.

'But I'd be game for a pint next Friday, if you've the time.'

'I don't think I'm too booked out.'

'Hear how you get by with Willie.'

They shook hands in the car, elbows bumping armrests and windows. Old Callum got out and lights flashed as he got into his car. The slick orange reflections on the wet road reminded Calum of the club lights on the body glitter.

'Vil-ni-us,' he said, in three distinct syllables.

Then Old Callum's car was gone and he sat for a while as the rain passed through.

Julie Rea
CANNIBALS

My dad reeked of rollup cigarettes and Old Spice aftershave, but there was always a faint trace of something else. Something mangy. Feral. His fingers were filthy, and he liked to scrape the oily muck from underneath his thumbnail, then flick the dirt onto our shabby living room carpet. He had a homemade tattoo on his forearm of a dagger with a coiled rattlesnake. I watched one rainy afternoon as he sat at the kitchen table and burned a sewing needle with a lighter, dipped the tip in ink, before roughly poking it onto the shaved patch of pink skin on his arm. His veins looked like blue and purple cables. When I think of him now, I don't see his face, it's that shitty tattoo I remember.

Every Saturday afternoon, while my mum cleaned offices in a business park, my dad – grisly and hungover – would make a breakfast of greasy bacon and rubbery fried eggs. The crusted dishes were left stacked high in the sink, and then we'd get the bus into town. I always wanted to go to the pet store to feed the guinea pigs but, ignoring my pleas, he dragged me to WH Smith instead. I aimlessly lurked the aisles, clutching my one-pound note, deciding what to buy – maybe a pineapple-shaped sharpener or a pencil eraser that looked like a frog? – while my dad stood at the magazine section, slowly skimming through copies of *Razzle*, *Mayfair* and *Escort*.

After a while, I'd hover sheepishly by his side, a rinse of clammy embarrassment spreading over my skin, until he shoved them back up on the rack, then we would leave the store, walking to the bus stop in a prickly silence.

I sometimes glimpsed the pictures in the magazines and their images scorched into my brain like a branding iron. It felt wrong he would look at those type of photos when I was with him, but to guess the reason why was a dark door that I kept sealed shut.

At the bus shelter, I perched on the raised bar, listlessly swinging my bare legs while he flirted with the teenage girls. They blushed at the attention until, seeing the leery glint in his eye, warily inched away from him. 'Prick teases,' he hissed under his breath, temper bristling, as I focused on a lump of hardened grey gum stuck to the ground, wishing I were anywhere else but there. I would grip the bar and put my head between my knees, a rush in my ears, like blood and fizzy cola all shook together. I imagined loosening my grip and falling onto the concrete, my head bursting open like a watermelon.

*

'He wanted to abort you,' my mum screeched at me one night, while they jabbed and volleyed insults and punches at each other across the dinner table. 'So did you,' he smirked. Crying, I ducked past them, skulking quickly along the hallway to my room, covering my ears as I slumped behind the bedroom door. A few days later, I looked up the word in a dictionary and something inside ruptured. It read – 'the deliberate termination of a human pregnancy.'

A human.

Me.

*

Underneath our house, behind a rotted wooden access panel, there was a narrow crawl space. It was mouldy and dank; the cinder blocks were always damp, and the air tasted soggy, like boiled leaves. It was my favourite place.

There was a grubby bare bulb hanging from a timber frame, which gave a tiny shock in my fingertips whenever I switched it on. I would take a clutch of books with me and old leather-bound photograph albums. I liked to lie flat on my stomach and flip through the pictures of them with me when I was a baby. They looked so young and happy then, I wished I could remember.

My mum was grinning in most of them, holding me in her arms or staring warmly down the lens at my dad, the photographer. I hardly ever saw her do that anymore so, on the rare occasions something amused her, I would capture her laughter and seal it up in empty glass jars in my mind to store away for later.

I saved them for days I got so sad it felt like a brick was jammed inside my rib cage. That's when I would close my eyes and unscrew one of those glass jars, listening hard to hear her high-pitched giggles, but then I'd slam it shut tight again, to preserve it, because there were hardly any jars left now.

I would lie in the crawl space until the light from the lone thin window above the entrance turned black, and the mildew and moisture had soaked into my pores, and I got wheezy. Sometimes it felt like my lungs were filling up with dirty water. Sometimes I liked to pretend I drowned.

*

My mum had only been working for a few months, ever since my dad lost his job at a local construction site. I heard her tell my aunt on the phone that the foreman had found him at eight a.m., passed out in a toilet cubicle, a half empty bottle of vodka beside him. They'd dragged him into the shower stall to wake him up. His clothes were still drenched when he arrived home later that day.

'Why are you wet?'

That was the first thing my mum had said to him, as he stood with water dripping from his cuffs onto the kitchen tiles with a *ploploplop.*

The second thing, with a dull dread, had been –

'Why aren't you at work?'

*

On those Saturday afternoons – once we got back from town and before my mum came home – my dad would run me a bath, leaning against the door jamb, smoking, and watching.

Always watching.

'Children are cannibals,' he'd sneer, 'but they eat you from the inside out.'

Then he'd take off all his clothes and get in the bath too.

Nicola Rose
EVEN BIRDS LIE

Her mother claimed her father looked like Bruce Willis. She could sometimes see it if maybe he had a different nose or if she paused the TV and his face was at the right angle and slightly blurred. Once on a school trip to London, she found the waxy version of the actor in the Hollywood Stars section of Madame Tussauds, wearing the classic dirty white tank top from *Die Hard*. She looked up at his familiar hard stare. Touched his oily arm, colder than she'd expected. He could have been real. The statue. The actor. The father.

It's his fault she's late for the interview. On the days she wakes up and he's there, in her head, everything feels slower, even time. When she finally arrives at the marketing firm, she's ten minutes late and her blouse is soaked through with sweat.

The marketing managers of the accountancy firm introduce themselves, but she forgets their names almost immediately. They sit on one side of a large desk. She sits on the other, so she is forced to stare at either the men or the clear blue sky outside of the floor-to-ceiling window behind them. The men are alike in build and age; old and tall with skinny arms and beer bellies straining against the tight buttons of their shirts. The one who led her in has tiny glasses that keep sliding down his oily face, so he has to readjust them with his knuckle. The other's hair is thinning on the crown of his head. He is writing something down on the clipboard on his lap. Already taking down first impressions, probably. Hair wild. Laddered tights. Slight smell of BO.

She is queasy from the buttery croissant she had for breakfast and the weird, chemical smell of the office. The Earl Grey tea she washed down the croissant with has left a furry layer on her tongue which she tries to scrape off with her teeth.

The glasses man shuffles some papers, slurps from a large mug, snorts and clears his throat, then looks up at her and smiles. His teeth are too small for his gums, and yellow.

'You know,' he says. 'We interviewed someone who looked exactly like you earlier.'

'Oh really?' she says. She doesn't know what else to say, so she just laughs.

'So, you studied English at university?' he asks, reading the information from his clipboard.

'Yes,' she says, straightening her spine and clasping her hands in her lap. She has the sudden urge to immediately justify this decision. Somewhere, her father asks why she never applied for the postgrad degree in teaching. He had a talent for making her feel bad about things she otherwise wouldn't feel bad about, like missing a perfect score on a test by a few marks or thinking vanilla was the best ice cream flavour. He was an ornithologist and she was always jealous of the delicate way he held the intricate marbled eggshells of golden eagles, studied strayed feathers plucked from peacocks, and the pages and pages he wrote on migration patterns and diets and how crows could be just as smart as seven-year-old children.

'You've had no previous marketing experience then?' the man says, peering at her over his glasses. Her pencil skirt is stuck to the back of her thighs, itching her skin. She knows when she stands up there will be a trail of sweat left on the plastic chair and down her bottom.

'No,' she swallows. The bald man's pen speeds across his paper, like he's excited to write down this crucial and humiliating information on her. Glasses nods, clears his throat in a way that sounds painful and makes her cringe.

'Why do you think you're the most suitable candidate for this job, then?' he asks.

This question isn't from the clipboard. It feels more like an accusation. She bites the inside of her cheek to jumpstart her brain. Why is she the most suitable for this job? Her knee bounces up and down. Her father would say she isn't, so that's what she says.

'Excuse me?' Glasses says. She scratches the back of her hot neck, finds a bump, tender and raised.

'I'm probably not the most suitable candidate for the job. I could be, though, depending on who else you interview.'

The men look at each other and laugh. She is attracted to them. The realisation of it almost makes her burst out laughing too. She pinches the lump on her neck between her finger and thumb and thinks of her ex. He has a receding hairline now and his sideburns grow all the way down to his chin. She knows this because he's begun uploading videos of himself onto the internet, playing video games, and she likes to watch them, usually late at night, on a private browser so there's no record of it in her search history. It's oddly satisfying to watch him sitting in his house alone and talking to the camera like there are hundreds of people watching when she knows there are only four, and she's one of them. It makes her feel better about herself. It's always strange seeing him again, even stranger hearing his voice; in the videos he pronounces certain words differently, sharpening his Ts and putting emphasis on vowels in a way she's never heard him do before. It makes her feel sick. It makes her want to crawl through the screen and scrape her fingernails down his face and screech into his eardrums, 'Who are you? This isn't you. I know it's not you, and you know it's not you, so why are you talking like that you fake fucking prick?'

Glasses says something that she has to ask him to repeat. He rhymes off another generic question about a time she's had to work effectively in a team, and she makes up a story about taking control during a busy period at the café she worked in when she was seventeen, even though she did all of her shifts with just one other person who never said a word, and they would have fewer than ten customers the whole day. The balding man scribbles and scribbles on the clipboard. She hides a yawn behind her hand.

'Anything else you'd like to say? Anything you want to ask us?'

She pauses, holds the air in her throat while she really thinks about this question.

'Do you know blue jays can do great impressions of hawks?' she says. She read it in one of her father's books.

Neither of them had expected her to say anything. The balding man stops scribbling. His pen hovers over his notepad as he looks at her for the first time since she sat down.

'Pardon?' Glasses says.

'Blue jays. Birds,' she says. 'It's so all the other birds think there's a predator nearby and fly away, and the blue jays can eat all the food for themselves.'

The two men stare at her, then at each other.

'Are there other animals that can make noises that sound like other animals?' she asks. 'Any other birds?'

There's silence, then the balding man speaks for the first time in the half hour since she sat down. 'Parrots?' he says, his voice cracking.

'Oh, of course!' she says. 'Parrots! How stupid of me. Did you know they can speak to humans because they want to be sociable? They want to fit in. They repeat human noises because they see people as part of their flock.'

Another awkward silence. There's a coffee stain on the collar of Glasses's shirt. His forehead is glittering with sweat. She thinks ahead a week; coming in for her first day preened and plucked, wearing a tight skirt and a shirt that's unbuttoned just enough to show some cleavage. She imagines Glasses leaning over her desk to get a glance of her breasts, his breath strong like coffee and whatever he'd had for breakfast that morning.

'That's quite sad, isn't it?' she says.

'You know, I think the person we interviewed earlier, the one who looked like you, was a lot more suitable for the job.'

'Oh, yes,' she says, as if she knows exactly what he's talking about. Yes, of course they were.

When she stands up there's a wet line on the plastic of the chair and she catches Glasses staring at it. They each shake her hand on the way out, saying they'll be in touch soon. She tries not to let the weight of her body pull her down to the floor. She presses the button for the elevator and waits. There's an itch on her neck again, where the lump is. She scratches it, squeezes, feels something slip out of her skin and between her fingers. A tiny grey feather. Its veins are tussled, ragged, wet with blood.

When her father died, she couldn't picture his face without thinking first of Bruce Willis, like some kind of father-celebrity hybrid where she couldn't tell the two apart. It was strange and infuriating to hear her mother stand up at his funeral and talk about how good a man he was when she'd had to listen to her call him every synonym for dick that she knew. After the service, old men who she figured out to be his colleagues came up to her and sandwiched her hands between their hairy, wrinkled fingers. They told her stories of what a kind, generous, intelligent addition her father had been to their lives. She wondered about this double life he led: prick and saint. Father and Hollywood actor.

His books are still in her flat, hidden between Eliot and Keats. She kept all of his unfinished papers on ospreys and red kites. Stole one of the peacock feathers and the skull of a bird with a beak as long as a pencil. She was desperate to find out what it was they did to warrant so much of his attention that she could not.

The elevator arrives with a chime. Its doors slide open and she is met with her own reflection in the mirror covering the back wall. When she was younger, she used to stare at herself in the mirror until her mother stared back. It used to startle her, how alike they were. She's glad that she never inherited any of her father's physical features but worries that means he's lurking somewhere else inside her. She told her ex this once. It was after the third time they'd had sex, and they hadn't bothered to close the curtains so the moon made his face grey and she had felt soft and vulnerable towards him. He said that she should try to be more empathetic towards him, as he was family after all. She never mentioned him again until her mother phoned to say that he had died.

The woman in the glass looks like a stranger now. Her skin is pink and her hair frizzes out from her temples. She has gotten so used to the image of herself in her head that when she does look in mirrors or windows or photographs, the sight of her own face takes her by surprise. She feels the same when she looks at other people, especially those she is supposed to know. When she meets up with friends it's like seeing two versions of the same person: the one in her head and the one there, in front of her. She stares at the structure of their bones, the pores on their nose, the flicks of ginger in their hair, and thinks, I have no idea who you really are. It is hard to remember people, faces, hard to tell who is real and who is made up. Dead relatives, kids she went to school with; it feels like she made them all up in her head.

She studies each part of her face, pokes the fatty parts of her cheeks and runs her finger down the hooked bridge of her nose. Has her hairline always been heart-shaped? Were her nostrils always different sizes? People always use that phrase – knowing something like the back of your hand. She's never been able to understand what it means. Does anyone actually know what the back of their hand looks like? If they don't, couldn't they just look down? And is it really knowing if you have to keep checking? Her hands are bumped and speckled, her fingers bony and curled, nails sharp like talons. She couldn't remember them looking like that this morning. Then again, she couldn't remember what they did look like before if not the way they looked now. They were her hands, the same ones that have always been attached to the end of her arms. How could she not know what they looked like?

She lifts her crooked hand to her face and the woman in the mirror copies. She makes shapes with her fingers, raises her arm, moving fast to catch herself out, but she follows her movements like they're in a synchronised routine. She sticks her tongue out, the woman does it too. She puts the feather under her nose and it looks like the woman in the mirror has a moustache. Together they pat their heads and rub their bellies like a pair of schoolgirls. She pushes her face against the glass and stares into her own eyes. Who are you? she thinks. Who is this person?

She gets off the elevator, the feather still gripped tight in her fist. She tiptoes out of the building so no one notices her. She tries her best to act like she doesn't exist. She floats down the street, her body made of air, her toes barely touching the ground.

That is when she sees herself. Not in a mirror or window. She is across the street inside a café, ordering a croissant and an Earl Grey tea. She knows that it's a croissant and an Earl Grey tea because the person ordering it is her. She has the same dark hair and polka-dot blouse, but something about her is different. The woman is breathtaking, not because of any of her physical features, but because she holds herself straight and tall like successful people who have nothing to worry about do. But it couldn't be herself. That was impossible. If the person in front of her was herself, so solid and real, then what did that make her? They meet eyes, and she waves like an old friend she hadn't expected to see. She looks down at her hand, the one gripping the feather and the hand is not the one she knows. Her skin is black and wrinkled, nails three inches longer, splitting at the tips.

Neil Gordon Shaw
THE BETTER STORY

Her dad's place is – *quelle surprise* – in a loser ex-council estate of grey pebble-dash semis at the edge of town . . . monster trampolines in small, overgrown front gardens; old Escorts on bricks in driveways; packs of seven-year-old oiks, barechested at nine in the morning on this fine July day. Not dissimilar to where Nicole Owen's parents lived, in that shithole town in north Wales.

And, ladies and gentlemen, we have a result . . . no motor parked outside number seventy-two! Never thought I'd be buzzing to be in fucking Derby but it's always a thrill to steal a march. Something tells me some dozy twats will be camped outside her boyfriend's bedsit in Tower Hamlets – probably her mum's gaff in Luton too. Got to do your research, gents.

Takes a second ring on the bell before the door's opened to reveal . . . da-da-*da-aa* . . . none other than the lady herself, Alexandra DeCruz. (Real name – don't laugh – Sophie Crichton.)

She ain't looking great.

When I saw her on the telly last night, I thought, *Well, I'd do her, given half a chance.* Maybe a shade over-endowed in the chin department for a wannabe pop star but a lot to like – bit dirty-looking, natural blonde, just the right side of chunky. Superb rack. This morning though, I'm impressed she's got the balls to answer the door, to be honest – standing there, red-eyed, nose like fucking Rudolf, mascara smudged down her pale cheeks with all the elegance of skidmarks in your bloomers. The girl's obviously been snivelling her way through the Kleenex. And who can blame her? Not every night you make a total cunt of yourself on national TV.

'Jack Verity,' I say, displaying the credentials. '*News on Sunday.*'

She sniffs, runs the back of her hand across her nose, then says: 'You think I want to speak to a newspaper after what they've just written about me?'

Her tone's not aggressive or whiny – more ironic, which is kind of surprising given how she looks. There's a flicker of spirit, too, in the way she holds my gaze. And the lady has a point – the coverage is bad – 'Alex DeMenter!' is a typical headline. But hey, let's look on the bright side – it's not as bad as it's going to be tomorrow . . . Today's papers will have gone to print shortly after last night's programme – just enough time to run the basic story on an inside page with a few stills from the show. But with the socials in meltdown and Miss DeMenter being talked about in every town in the land, tomorrow will be the moment for the high-profile, in-depth spread with all the juicy background. And yours truly is just the man to deliver it.

'Yeah, well, I'm from a different paper, love. The *Sunday*'s nothing to do with the *Daily*. My paper wants to give you the chance to put your side of the story.'

You always wonder whether they're going to let you in. The smart ones generally don't, although the story always gets written. But whatever Sophie Crichton has going for her, it's probably not brains, right?

She hesitates, then says, 'Long as you go easy on me. I'm feeling pretty bruised right now.'

You don't say.

'Sure.'

'I can't believe all this is happening, to be honest.'

And in we go, into a boxy, beige front room, with standard issue three-piece suite, coffee table and huge telly – a room with all the personality of a cash dispenser. It's less of a tip than you might expect from someone whose life has just gone tits up but that doesn't stop her mumbling, 'Excuse the mess,' and scurrying about picking up discarded tissues.

For a moment, I think, *Hello? Little lady's all on her lonesome.*

You wouldn't believe how many people, including young females on their own, just wave you inside at moments of crisis, almost like you're one of the emergency services. But then a noise upstairs and 'I'll get my dad – he's in the shower.'

'Couldn't have a coffee, love, could I? Milk, two sugars?'

Once she's fucked off, I take a few pics on the SLR. Go back a few years and I'd have had a pap with me, taking care of that side of things. These days I'm a one-man band. I snap the two shelves of family photos: what looks like big sis – decidedly undoable . . . dad – a gently inflated Tom Jones lookie-likey, greying, with a goatee . . . and our songbird herself – mic in hand in a couple of pictures, on some stage, doing her thing as an Eva Carnethy tribute act. Then the shelf above, three trophies for – I kid you not – her singing. Pride of place goes to a cup from Butlins in Bognor Regis. The little shrine reminds me of the one I saw last year in Nicole Owen's parents' place. Like that, it's a testament to that most pathetic and dangerous of things: parental delusion.

The coffee table is covered with the tabloids – the scene, no doubt, of a terrified and increasingly horrified scouring this morning. I clock the *Sun*'s front page – half of it's taken up with a picture of the Duchess of Cambridge, with the caption 'In the Pink!' – and I'm reminded, as I often am, of my first editor, Harry Dawson, a Jock and as old-school as they come. I hadn't been in the door a week when Harry imparted a little of his wisdom: 'The pictures of Queenie or the fragrant princess on the front pages every other day?' he said, over a pint. 'You might think it's all trivial tat, son. But you'd be dead wrong. Because what those pictures say to the Great Unwashed is, "Bow down to your betters. Don't ever forget your fucking place." Which, for the half-dozen people who own the British press, is the most important message of all.'

I hear the floorboards creaking in the hall before he appears – Señor DeCruz, a mug in each hand. Did I say a '*gently* inflated Tom Jones'? Scratch that – cunt's fucking vast, must be twenty stone. The loose-fitting black shirt, size of a sail, is fooling no-one. The girl of the moment brings up the rear, sipping her coffee.

Still a bit red-eyed, but she's scrubbed up nicely. Gone are the grey
trackies and crumpled t-shirt she opened the door in. Now it's
jeans, white shirt, hair tied up, mascara cleaned away and reapplied.
You can tell that before long she'll be just another beefy horror
at the bingo – that's her destiny, it's in the genes. But right now, at
twenty-one, girl's in her very fleeting prime.

'There you go,' says Man Monster, handing me the mug. Thick
Brummie accent – in both senses. She's got a bit of a twang but he
makes her sound like Camilla Parker-Fucking-Bowles. 'Our Soph
says you're going to let her tell the story of what really happened
on that bloody show. Is that true?'

'Absolutely.'

We do the introductions – he's Dave – and I shake his podgy
hand, still repellently warm and baby-like from the shower, then
he wedges his huge arse between the arms of the easy chair by the
window, while daughter perches on the edge of the sofa next to
me. It's real coffee, which surprises me. I'd have bet the farm on
the DeCruzes being an instant household.

'Don't suppose there's any money in it for her?' he asks. As they
all do. 'Least the poor girl deserves after what she's been through.'

I smile sympathetically. 'None of the papers would pay a fee for
this type of story, I'm sorry to say. But I guess that setting the record
straight would bring its own reward, right?'

They both agree it would.

I place my recorder on the table.

There are going to be four acts in this little play of ours.

Act One – the snaps. Her, then him, then together.

'Just be yourselves,' I say. 'No need to pose or smile. I suspect
you've got every right to be pissed off.'

I'm hoping for psychotic but settle for sullen. Good to get these
in the bag at this point in proceedings. I resist the temptation to
ask her to undo a couple of buttons, give us a glimpse of bra. Eyes
on the prize, Verity.

Act Two is 'context'.

'This is just a chance to get to know you better, love, before we get down to what happened. Understand the real you.' Consummate professional that I am, nary a hint of a smile shades my lips as I say this.

Context is what I'm here for. And I'm forensic: birth, parents, sister, friends, boyfriends, school, any fights, any bullying or being bullied, singing competitions, any medical conditions that might help readers relate to her – anxiety, depression, anorexia, maybe?

She's a bit cagey at first but then opens up. As I expected she would – ain't nothing needy little wannabes love more than attention.

'It's always been my number one dream to be a singer,' she enlightens me. 'I've sung every day since I was eight.'

From time to time a piss-weak smile even makes an appearance, such as when she recalls spotting her parents by the side of the stage when she won the Butlin's singing competition.

'My dad's doing this little, like, victory dance! It's the only time I've ever seen him like that.'

Dave the Rave has the decency to look suitably embarrassed at this grotesque image.

She's still fragile but the girl's regrouped since she opened the door to me. She's thinking it's only half time – that she might have got utterly humped by the press in the first half but she can still pull it back in the second.

Her context is mostly boring as fuck, of course, but there's a lot in there I can use. And two little nuggets: how singing has helped her battle depression – always useful, the stench of mental illness. And – even better – a couple of fights at high school with the ringleader of a group who had been bullying her.

'The bullying stopped after the second one,' she says, wiping her nose with a tissue. 'It taught me the importance of standing up for yourself.'

Rather wonderfully Señor lets slip the ringleader's name in passing: Beverley Douglas.

And then we're on to Act Three – Our Soph's experience on *Talent Factory* – and it's her turn to get forensic. She's keen that I understand exactly what happened and when, like she's giving a police statement that's going to clear her name. A statement that contains no real surprises, of course. I might not have known the details but I was sure about the gist: she got shafted. And pretty artistically as it turns out . . . Instructed to show up at the studios ridiculously early. Kept in some holding pen for hours on end with no access to food. Told the audition wouldn't go ahead unless she dropped the Nina Simone number she'd chosen and did an Eva Carnethy song instead – even although she was trying to get away from the tribute act thing. And then, when her song finished, the unimpressed judges asking her why she chose an Eva Carnethy song if she wanted to move away from being a tribute artist, suggesting, as they unanimously voted to reject her, that she should have opted for a more adventurous song . . . something by Nina Simone perhaps?

Her freak-out was TV gold – fury, tears, yelling, swearing, throwing the mic down, storming off, storming back on again, storming off again, shoving the camera man, which resulted in him falling and needing stitches. An off-the-charts tantrum from a half-demented low-rent diva.

'I shouldn't have reacted the way I did,' she says, eyes on the floor. 'It was out of character. I'm really ashamed. But I'd been waiting for months – years – for that opportunity. And they deliberately wrecked it, made me look like an idiot, humiliated me, in front of millions of people.'

She drains her coffee, places the mug on the table.

'In the edit it looked even worse than it was. They completely cut anything I'd said about it being a set-up. And in reality when I came off stage, the camera man followed me for minutes while I was having this, like, total breakdown. I was begging him to stop and then I finally snapped and pushed him. But the way they edited it, it was like I'd run off stage and immediately attacked him.'

I don't doubt she's telling the truth.

'They just completely manipulated me from start to finish.'

I nod sympathetically. I'm thinking: of course they manipulated you, you silly little tart. What were you expecting? An earnest reproduction of your instantly forgettable performance? They're about entertainment, the story, ratings. Not dissimilar to my line of work, as it happens.

And then we're finished with Act Three.

I click the recorder off.

Now, for a lot of journos, that's job done. Off they'll pop, with a smile and a handshake. Often before totally screwing the person over in the paper the next day. But I'm rather partial to the more direct approach.

So, time to shift gear. Time for Act Four.

'Well, that's all very good. But something you've got to understand.'

I pause for dramatic effect.

'What counts is not what you've said, it's what we say you've said. And it's not what happened, it's what we say happened.'

They're both looking at me, working to catch up, aware that something's changed, and not in a good way. No matter how many times I give this speech, I always get a little buzz.

Daddy DeCruz recovers first. 'How do you mean?'

'How I mean is this: my paper will be going with the *Talent Factory* version of events, not yours.'

She's gazing at me wide-eyed, mouth open. In the space of maybe three seconds, disbelief shades into horror then into panic. When she's able to make a sound, it comes out as a wail: 'What for?'

I get to my feet and pocket the recorder. 'Better story, love.'

Buffalo Boy is sitting up, clenching the armrests. 'Is this for real?' he says, voice and – unless I'm very much mistaken – hackles raised.

'Oh, totally.'

Her eyes are welling up.

'Please.'

She almost whispers it. You can see she's about to go under. That flicker of spirit from earlier? It ain't flickering no longer.

'Sorry, love. That's what's happening. I'd fasten your seat belt, if I were you.'

She dissolves, buries her face in her hands, starts sobbing, babbling about not believing it, about it not happening.

He's on his feet, impressively quickly, all things considered.

'GET THE FUCK OUT MY HOUSE!'

Surprising how loud his voice is in the little room.

I sling my jacket over my shoulder. I'm not intimidated. I'm in way better shape than this silage heap.

'You people are fucking vultures!' He hasn't advanced from in front of the chair but he's literally wobbling with rage. 'Should be a law against what you're doing!'

For a moment I think about taking a leaf out of Harry's book, educating the fucker, asking him why he supposes there isn't a law against it, why there never has been, never will be; putting him straight on how the Great British Press does far too valuable a job protecting Power – 'attack dogs patrolling the periphery,' as old Harry put it – to ever be restrained. And how the people who run this great country couldn't give less of a fuck about us flogging papers on the back of stories about losers like Dave Crichton and his talentless, deluded, ten-a-penny offspring.

But then again, why bother?

Instead, a thought occurs to me – bit of a naughty one, I have to confess.

I turn around, Columbo-like, as I reach the open living room door, and say, 'Oh, Sophie, love?'

She lifts her head up from her hands. Her face is quite the picture. Wet cheeks. Puffy red eyes. We're back to square one with the mascara, I'm afraid.

She's looking at me like a wounded animal – fearful, diminished, but also with a glimmer of hope – like I might, against all odds, be about to make things better. Not proud of it, but I can feel myself getting hard.

'This is just the way of it. And I'm not pretending it's going to be easy, living down something like last night. Welsh girl fucked up like you on the same show last year. Not quite as violently, right enough. Nicole Owen was her name. Why don't you google what happened to her?'

Buddha Boy makes a sound that belongs in the animal kingdom and lunges towards me but I stand my ground, sticking out my hand like I'm a cop halting the traffic. He stops, wild-eyed and red-faced. I can hear his breathing, feel it on my fingers.

I'm aware of her sobbing again too, face back down in her hands. It's quieter than before but also, you get the impression, deeper.

'You know, Dave,' I say, my hand still raised. 'It would really put the cherry on the cake if I could say I was attacked by the dad. You know, "Like father, like daughter"? Attacked by the dad and pressing charges. Black eye in the paper.'

There's a hint of fear in his eyes now. Then something like defeat.

'Just leave,' he says quietly.

I park at the entrance to the estate, get on the socials, make a couple of calls, and hey presto, we've got a Beverley Douglas, also twenty-one, works at Specsavers in – what are the chances? – central Derby. I have three hundred notes in the wallet that says Miss Douglas will be more than agreeable to telling me all about her ordeal at the hands of Alex DeMenter.

I can sense the piece coming together now. As I drive towards the town centre, I run a possible opening around in my mind: 'Alexandra DeCruz's violent meltdown on Friday's *Talent Factory* brought back traumatic memories for one young woman who's all too familiar with the wannabe star's volcanic temper . . .'

And then I can't help imagining the first words of another story, a future one, bigger, more of an earner: 'Just nine months after *Talent Factory* hopeful Nicole Owen took her own life, the hit show was last night reeling from the suicide of another painfully young contestant. Tragic Sophie Crichton was only twenty-one when . . .'

Probably never happen, of course. But you got to admit, it is the better story.

Amy Stewart
THE ORANGE

The cool air from the supermarket fan felt like a kiss. It had been a long time since anyone had kissed Simone like that – not lightly on the cheek or even deeply on the mouth, but down the slope of her neck and then across her shoulders, the kind of kiss that asks the body to respond. She stood in the doorway for a long moment, under the attention of the fan, the sweat on her skin beginning to dry. She imagined crystals forming, making salt flats in the hollows of her collarbones.

A man behind her said something (maybe 'excuse me', but Simone didn't speak good enough Spanish to know) and moved past her into the supermarket. The backs of his calves were tanned a deep gold, the muscles in them obvious, curving into definition with every step. Simone wanted to trace the lines with her fingertips. It was the kind of day when everything, everyone, was beautiful. Simone hadn't felt that for a long time, either.

The supermarket was small, dusty, and dark after the ferocity of the sun outside. Flies swarmed around the dim ceiling lights and a radio blared from behind the counter. There was something desperate about that elongated vibrato, the twinkling minor key, and Simone knew it would be a love song.

She wandered the aisles, wondering what to buy. The choice to extend her stay had brought plenty of these new decisions with it. She'd exhausted the staples left for her by the villa owner that morning, eating the last of the jam straight from the jar, legs dangling over the balcony. There were only a few widely spaced bars to constitute a railing. Paul would have called it unsafe. Simone revelled in that fact, added it to the internal list of things she could do now that she couldn't before. *Drink beer at ten a.m. Take two-hour naps. Rent a villa with a death trap for a balcony.*

She found herself standing by the bread. Bread was a sensible choice, something to soak up all that Ambar Especial. She didn't know what would taste good, knew that it didn't really matter. She kept forgetting to eat properly until the middle of the night anyway, when she'd sit, feeling kind of dull but still alert, in front of the TV and eat whatever was closest and easiest. She settled for a bag of limp-looking slices, knowing Paul would never have chosen it. She was pretty sure Paul hadn't eaten pre-sliced bread in a bag since 2005. She added it to her list. *Buy shit bread if I want.*

Simone moved on to the alcohol aisle. Wine was so much cheaper here than at home, the beer barely cost more than bottled water. She picked up a red with a colourful label, rolled the cool glass across her chest, sighing in the way that heat makes you sigh. At the end of the aisle, the man with the golden calves was watching her. When she looked up, he turned quickly away, though it was with the kind of smile that made Simone's stomach twist. He had strong-looking forearms, the hair there thick as thatch. She studied the bottle of wine in her hand. She used to drink herself dizzy on a Friday night just so she could let Paul touch her. It hadn't felt that dramatic at the time, just part of the routine, like putting out the bins on Wednesday night or clicking on the kettle. Now, though, she could feel her body loosening, opening, responding to the faintest suggestion of touch. A woman appeared at the end of the aisle, placed her hand on the man's elbow. They moved away together, and Simone put the wine in her basket.

The fruit aisle was better stocked than the others: a cascade of lemons the size of apples back home, pulpy melon slices wrapped in cling film, unnameable things with reptilian scales. Simone let her hands dance across the skins. Waxy, firm, soft, sagging. Straight after the separation, she'd seen Paul's face in everything, determined each time that it was uncanny and predestined, like the people who saw Jesus in their toast. Even while knowing it could be nothing more than pattern recognition – than seeing a face every day then suddenly not seeing it at all, than a mind trying to fill the blanks – she still lingered longer over the shape of wisping clouds, the arrangement of cereal grains in her abandoned bowls. She could always find something: the cleft in his chin, the sweep of his hair. She searched for his face now in the dimpled textures of the fruit, found nothing. It left an emptiness in the pit of her belly, a pulling, more urgent than hunger.

Simone picked up three lemons, two bananas and one large orange, unblemished and vivid. Her mouth was dry, and she imagined the release of the juice underneath the pith, sweet and sticky.

When she took her shopping to the counter, the love song on the radio had been replaced by something with an earthy beat and a sultry voice slipping around over the top. *Lento, lento,* it pleaded, which Simone knew meant, *slow, slow.*

She'd chosen Spain because they'd never been here together. It seemed, when booking the tickets, that they'd been almost everywhere else. A tangle of memories stretched across the globe: missed flights from Copenhagen to Stockholm, pyramid tours in Egypt, cold wine in France. So many of them were good memories, forming a shared history they often dipped into at dinners, parties, occasions. Spain was unsullied and unshared. There was also the fact that her grandfather had been Spanish, had taught her spiky-sounding words on his knee – *naranja, manzana, cereza* – and so it had felt like somewhere private and rooted. Spain was a place for making new memories, ones that felt all the more hard-won for having been made alone. Simone created a new list in her head, things she could remember later that would bring her back here, to a time she'd been brave: *the way the breeze sweeps across the sea, like fingers across skin; the specific colour of the cobbles in town, like tarnished copper; how the oranges smell: sweet, bitter, strong.*

The cashier was looking at Simone with a deep line between his eyebrows, and she realised she had the orange lifted to her nose, had closed her eyes to smell it without the rest of the world crowding in. The shop was quiet now, the couple having left, and out in the square, the water fountain trickled on and on. Simone liked the way the cashier was looking at her, the way the light

from the door made a sunbeam of his cheekbone. He was looking
at her in a way that was not polite, not kind – but as though
he wanted to bite her and really make it hurt. Paul used to look
at her like that, in the beginning. Simone wanted someone to
always be looking at her like that. To make the muscles of her
stomach feel taut and strong, to make her feel as though she could
barely swallow with the thickness in her throat. To make her feel
young – Simone wasn't old, but she'd been younger – to make her
feel wanted, and alive.

She took her turn to look at him. He was more boyish than she'd
first thought – all long limbs and graceful features, maybe early
twenties. His skin was rich and unmarked, his hair unwieldy, a
mess of brown curls.

'Anything else?' he asked, motioning to the cigarettes, the chewing
gum. His accent wrapped around the English words like entwined
legs in a bed.

Simone shook her head. She was still holding the orange. She
could feel the scratch of sand between her feet and flip flops, the
knot of her bikini top leaving a red mark on the back of her neck.
She pushed her thumb into the top of the orange. It resisted, the
skin bending and straining, then finally yielding, a trickle rising
up and running down the side. The cashier watched her, wordless.
There was an advert on the radio now, a woman speaking fast and
loud. Simone's fingers felt capable as she started to unwrap the
orange, never breaking his gaze, dropping pieces of peel all over
the counter. When she'd finished, she collected and pocketed them,
knowing she'd never get the smell out of the cotton. Her fingers
were slicked with juice, and the peeled orange sat on the counter
between them. There was something heavy-lidded about the boy
now, and Simone marvelled at the way it seemed to transform him,
like she'd unlocked something in him without saying anything all.
This was old language, she knew. This was how bodies talked to
each other. Her body – her *body*, she reminded herself, because

sometimes it was as though she'd forgotten she had one at all – her body had so much to say.

Simone removed a single segment of orange, and it made a sound like a whisper as it pulled away from the whole. It was plump and untorn. She offered it to the boy, watched his eyes travel from her lips to her fingers. She placed it on his tongue, felt the warmth there, the way he closed his lips to catch her fingers between them for half a second. He chewed slowly, smiling, and Simone unpeeled another segment for herself. She felt the fragile roughness on her tongue, followed by the explosion of liquid. She closed her eyes to concentrate on it, on everything contained in a single moment. The cool air, the radio, the sweetness, the throb of another body close by, the fountain, on and on.

When Simone opened her eyes, the cashier was still watching her, wiping juice from the corner of his mouth. There was a tiny scar on his chin, and his eyes were the colour of river water. He was so beautiful. The day was so beautiful. He leaned forward and said something low and heavy, and Simone didn't know if it was in English or Spanish.

She knew what would happen next, if she wanted it to, if she decided: the way she'd climb over the counter to him, into the darkness of a back room, her body compressed by his, those tanned hands on both her hips, the scent and taste of one orange on two breaths.

She could pinpoint the exact moment the attraction she'd felt for Paul had solidified into something deeper and more permanent. It was brought about by a strange, silly combination of things: two shots of sambuca at a uni bar, him wearing a bright red clown wig, eighties pop playing in the background. The shot had gone down the wrong way, too fast, too strong, and she'd felt the liquid rising again, had groped for the bar. Paul scooped her hair into one hand and put the other on the small of her back, smile fading. 'It's all right,' he'd said, and Simone had not so much heard as seen the words on his lips, seen a man who didn't care what he, or they, looked like to anyone else. Seen the kindness at the core of him. Not that any of it had been enough, in the end. Even the kindest person can still carve pieces out of you, given sufficient time.

The cashier was still staring at Simone, low-lidded, head tilted in suggestion. She shook her head, knowing he'd understand. He shrugged, becoming more alert with the slow dissolving of desire. He grinned at her, blew air out through his lips like he'd just seen something incredible. Simone thanked him, handed over a jangle of coins and lifted her bag of shopping, leaving the rest of the orange on the counter. As she left the supermarket, she could hear the radio whine with the onset of another love song.

Lynn Valentine
A CAR DRAWS UP

Those three long weeks she went out walking,
touring the broken lanes of her childhood,
running rows of fragile houses, reconstructing

slums from condemnation: low windows,
the cracked front step, cooling cinders in the grate,
stones pouching her cheeks as she lies in her last bed.

She sits in the palace of the forgotten cinema,
recites *We are minors of the ABC*, feels
her brothers' hands in hers, though both are nowhere
near, blesses them for trying to be good.

She is thirsty, so thirsty but can't find
a tap or the dirty river she used to fish in.
She rests in a garden of yews, snow hardening.

Her mother drives a car past the garden gate,
her mother like her, who never learned to drive.
Her mother brakes – *in you get lass, it's time.*

Ryan Van Winkle
THE RUINED HOUSES OF THIS VILLAGE REMIND ME

No, she said, this isn't a house. You can turn
the bathroom light off and on all night
if you want to. It won't change how I see
maple leaves stretching out our broken panes,
roots striving through linoleum or flashes
of our bed covered in moss, bugs burrowing

in the least romantic way. The future made her tired, she said,
it was all impossible – keeping sheets white, pillows plump.

Let's say *we'll do the dishes, put them in their place.*
Let's say *let them crust and hurl them at the stars.*

FLIGHT PATH AWAY

My father calls me by my brother's name so often
I lose my face. The map on the back of this seat reminds me
wherever I am, his tomatoes will thicken into red bruises
and I will leave. One day, he too

will lighten and lift from the earth. For my whole life
I will be able to look at a map, lay my finger where I was made.
There will be a final leg, a one-way trip towards a time when
no map will help me plot a way back home.

Katie Webster
SKIN TASTE TOUCHING

ONE

I've a song.

Songs are nice. Songs sing words and words sing songs and I can sing a string of things and know that they are nice. A song is nearly one of the nicest things ever. Don't you think?

I sing in my head. I always sing in my head. I don't sing out loud. Bits do get through though sometimes; bits break the breaches and tsunami out of my mouth, like sugar spilling from the bag dropped by mistake and right before the cook-wifie's clout.

I sing rhymes and I sing chimes, and I sing my echolalia hiding heartfelt hefty words. If I had a girl I'd call her Echolalia, Laila for short, and she'd call me Mum, and we could sing our songs together instead of on our own. I don't have a girl, and I never will. I don't sing out loud, and I'd thought in my head that I never would. But one day. One day I think today is the day to change that.

I've a song.

One of the cleaner-wifies stays back extra every day, to sit with a boygie who sits. Who twitches, flails, gurns, drools, smiles, grimaces. Who grimaces, smiles, drools, gurns, flails, twitches. That's it. He's riddled by, ridden by, involuntary tics, rictus of the lips, spasms of the hips. He sits – windswept, kyphotic, scoliotic, lordotic – twisted in the grip of a brain and body that just . . . sit.

She stays back extra, after her shift, sits in close, and she . . . sings to him. Sings with him. He makes his noises, his hics and his pips, and she . . . echoes them back. And then he echoes her! He does. They'd tell you there's no way he could do that. They'd tell you he's not capable of that. But he does.

The nasty nursies tut and sneer. *Who does she think she is? What does she think she's doing? Is that even appropriate?* They would never. And I would tell them. I would tell them *don't you dare* and *who exactly do you think* you *are?* And *she's worth ten of you* and I would triumph in their small-mind blinking, telt-off shrinking. I would. I'd defend her to the end.

But I don't need to because she is not embarrassed. Their spite is water off a duck's back. Have you ever seen a duck that's lost its waterproofing? When we used to have the hospital farm here, we used to have ducks. We used to collect their cool blue eggs still warm from their backsides. But a duck that's lost its waterproof coating is a pathetic thing. Shite mats in its feathers. It tries and it tries, but there's no way it can preen it out. Eventually it'll die of it. That is what they hope for, the nursies. They want their sneers to clag in the cleaner-wifie's feathers and chill her to the bone. Kill off the warmth of her. But she is waterproof. She is bulletproof. She is spiteproof. She is as beautiful as a sleekit duck. She is as warm as a duck's bum. She does not give a fuck. About the harsh words of nursies.

She and the young man who sits, they riff, backwards and forwards, they craft a thing of beauty together. It is a relationship. It is a two-way conversation of squeaks and croons. They pass the baton, of echo and mimic, of listening and heard. It is a conversation that means everything. It is kindness and connection, respect and affection. They only have eyes and ears for each other.

He smiles when she's with him, he laughs when they sing their song. And it is not a rictus, it is not a tic, it is not an empty spasm of muscles, 'told by an idiot, signifying nothing.' It is a smile that shines out of his eyes. And she, she shines right back at him.

I've a song

I say. My song that's been held in my head so long. My inside song where nice things string and Laila's warm wee hand holds mine.

That song where up till now only jigged-jagged ragged-sounds have ever made it out. But today is different. Today the right words come, and I get them out and I say, I say

I've a song.

The boygie who sits, he flicks, he drips, he clicks . . . and he twists . . . to make a space for me in their duet. And a smile flits with the spittle and fits, and he is happy to share her with me. His eyes say *join us.*

But she hasn't seen me, she's facing the other way so she can't, so I reach out and I touch her on the arm.

I've a song.

I say, ready, to meet them halfway, to blend my song with theirs, heart open, all hope and –
– she flinches. And shakes off my hand, like I'm a splash of something dirty.

Hands to yourself please, no touching.

is all she cares to say to me. I retreat, like an arm from a needle, like a mental one from a nurse. My song stays in my head. It's safer there.

TWO

The psychiatrist's new watch is gold, shiny yellow, with tiny links that sparkle in the sun. I'd like to slide my finger over those links, and feel the bump bump bump of them, as giddy as the cattlegrid at the end of the drive when we're leaving on a bus run.

This day, I set about it. I'm a dwalm with a plan. I sidle up. I feign to be much much less than I am.

He doesn't know, it would never even occur to him, what it is I'm up to, why I'm suddenly patting at his wrists, and looking for holding at his hands. I'm careful. I'm as non-threatening as I've learned to be. I play at being one of the cute-faced-dearies, all hugs and lovie-doves, so's I can get in close enough. I do it.

I plant my thumb on the face of his fancy watch.

He'll polish it eventually, like he polishes his spectacles, though not as often, hazing its surface – *hough* – with a heavy sigh of clever breath, then rubbing it sheeny shiny on a corner of a fresh clean handkerchief.

But that doesn't matter, because for now, and maybe even a day or two, if I'm lucky – am I lucky? – my print is there. My thumb whorls are skiting the glass face of his watch, and free to go wherever he goes.

He is perplexed by my behaviour. Wrong-footed, I can see. Me turning nice as a cute-faced-dearie, all touchy-feelie, it's not what anyone expects of me.

Maybe he's thinking, clocking the changes in my behaviour and assuming that they're signs of progress with the new meds. Crediting himself. It's what they do, isn't it; dispense meds. Take credit.

Or maybe he's not. Maybe he's fully occupied, minding on Jinty Mac in Admin and her babydoll nighties. Either way, I've got him caught with the wrong foot out, like a room full of us lot doing the hokey-cokey at the midsummer dance. All he can do is gently redirect me, verbal prompt me, back into line, *hands to yourself please, no touching*. But it's too little too late. I've got what I wanted.

So now my thumbprint tours the wards, like a VIP, a visitor, who gets a tour and gets to go home after. And I can feel the ice-smooth clean-ness of the watch-face still tingling on my skin. I carry it around with me for the rest of the day, cherishing it, and refusing to touch anything else with it, with that fleshy pad of thumb. It keeps me going through the whole day, through cuppateatime, through the long dead dull of afternoontime. None of the others

have it, this treasure, this skin taste of something clean and expen-
sive and free to leave.

I am special.

At timetomakedinnertime, it all goes wrong. I'm meant to be
chopping onions, but it's a hard thing to do without letting your
thumb touch something. You should try. I try a few different ways,
till I'm looking even more cack-handed than I usually do. And I
can't explain, can't say anything beyond, *Canna chop today, canna
chop, chop chop, chop chop, not today.*

The nursie and the cook-wifie take dim view of that, dim like
the dark corners of a low-grade ward. Dim in a way that doesn't
bear inspection. Doing our chores is required. Non-compliance is
not okay. The notes will say I *declined to participate.* But all the staff
know that that's code for *had the audacity to refuse.* Natural conse-
quences will be imposed. It's part of my behaviour support plan.

But that's okay. Because tonight my thumbprint will be leaving
this place. My thumbprint will be bumping over that cattlegrid
at the end of the drive, and going home with the psychiatrist.

THREE

That day, I take against the tea.

I canna hold it in, the feel, the clag of the milk and the sugar
swilling over my teeth, it's too much. I dump my cup down rough,
and crack it on the trolley, and do a bit of huffing and puffing
at the nursie coming at me with a handful of paper towels for
the slops.

It's not my fault she takes me all wrong. She says, *Go canny or
you know what you'll get*, and then, with a flick of her eyes and a
purse of her mouth, she tells her pal that I'm trouble. And both
their faces flush in the face of me.

And how dare they? How dare they take me for a mental one,
when I'm just expressing a fair dislike for something that I shouldna
have til swallow. It's only tea. Can I no say no til a foul-supped

cuppatea? And is this no exactly how they made it foul in the first place?

Her pal's delighted. She would be. It's been a boring week, long and boring and with no drama at all, and her pal's a nursie who likes a spot of drama. They're at me til hold my horses, while clipping their whips in my face, clipping their whips of warnings and trips, trips and jibs, jibs and jibes, all hid as help, they'll no let me hide. And then they say,

Hands to yourself please, no touching.

And I lose it. I canna hold it in. I start til screech and stamp, and whack my head, bash bash bash, till the blood is pulsing before my eyes, and a bump is building square flush and livid on the front of my brow, and I'm brinking til cowp into fury.

And then he's there. Staff Nurse William.

He's rushing in, sure as steam, and he's got me down in seconds, leaving bitch-face nursie and her pal both looking glad, and both looking scunnert, all at the same time cuz, *ha, she's got what was coming til her*, but it's over too soon, and all their drama's took already, whisked out from under them, just when it was meant til get good.

He's got me on the floor, in one of his 'hurt-free' holds, hurt free, we'll see, so long as you danna struggle.

I don't. I breathe. I don't want til, but I do it, I peek, up, intil his eyes. And he meets me half-way, and he sees. He sees all that I'm seeing and knowing and clocking in this place, all that I understand but shouldn't, understand under cover of stupid and glaikit and learning disability. He sees, that I clocked him a long time ago, and the glory glow that shines off him when it all kicks off. He sees that I'm bracing for him til hurt me now, and his eyes jolt like jaws do when the ECT switch gets flipped and

I wait for it.

I shut my eyes and squeeze them tight and wait for it. For the restraint to escalate, till it hurts, till I break, in an arm, in a bone, in the ligaments of my spirit. I wait till I break. With my eyes shut.

But it goes on too long, and I canna hold it in. After a second of that, or two, or three, I peek. And he's . . .

Meek.

He's backed off from the break and his eyes are on fire but they say *no*. They say *I am not that man. I am not that man who hurts for fun, who hurts these folk because he can.* His eyes say *no. That is not who I am.*

He picks me up nice, and he waves off the bitchies who're clamouring for jags and the consequences of my actions. He's saying, *she's fine, give her some space.* And he helps me til my feet, and

holds me, touching my arm,

light and steady and calm, until he asks me if I'm fine now. I say, *aye*, and I repeat it, *aye aye aye, fine now, fine now*, trying til hide my fear in echolalic speaking. And he nods, hot eyes easing, and suggests I go, *have a wee sit down in the other room, have a wee relax and a forget*, and I says, *aye aye, time oot, time oot*, and he guides me through til the other room and away from yon two bitchies, and he sits me doon, and he lets me be.

And as he's going, he says, *so you'll not be wanting a cuppatea then?* And I says, *no no no, no tea, no tea.*

And he grins, and I see that he's grinning, and so do I. And it's nearly nice. It's nearly one of the nicest things ever.

Jay Whittaker
MISTAKEN

I was full of it – sea-air, myself –
exhilarated to stride the cliff-top turf,
pocketing flat periwinkle shells,
brittle opalescence tossed aloft,
dashed on thin-bladed grass,
ready to join my collection –
cowries, pebbles, sea glass –
on my sand-dusted window sill.

The next morning, three shells vertical, cling
to my artfully draped bladderwrack frond.
There I was, fooling myself
they were already dead
not shrivelled in their spirals
to survive.

AN ABANDONED ICE CREAM VAN CONSIDERS
ITS POSITION AT MIDWINTER

One shove, decades ago,
plunged me headlong
down this steep, wooded bank.
I lie in pieces.

My radiator fractured,
pistons rust-crumpled.
Minnie Mouse fades and peels
from my pink side-panels.

Jabberwock trees, hold me
in your gnarled embrace.
I long for spring,
our green grave.

BIOGRAPHIES

Gail Anderson began storytelling as a stop-motion animator. She teaches creative writing at the University of Oxford, and is a 2023 Ignite Fellow with the Scottish Book Trust, working on a collection of interwoven short fictions based in south-west Scotland. She sails in the Firth of Clyde.

Nasim Rebecca Asl has been published in magazines such as *Poetry Wales*, *Modern Poetry in Translation* and *Gutter*, has performed across the UK, is a Scottish Book Trust New Writers Awardee and an Edwin Morgan Poetry Award shortlistee. Her debut pamphlet *Nemidoonam* was published by Verve Poetry Press in February 2023.

'S ann à Glaschu a tha **Shelagh Chaimbeul**. Chaidh Duais Ghàidhlig mar phàirt de Dhuaisean nan Sgrìobhadairean Ùra Urras Leabhraichean na h-Alba a bhuileachadh oirre ann an 2022.
Shelagh Campbell is a fiction writer from Glasgow. She was selected as the Scottish Book Trust's Gaelic New Writer Awardee for 2022.

Rachel Carmichael lives in Glasgow. Her stories have been published in *thi wurd*'s magazine and its anthology *Alternating Current*, *Northwords Now*, NFFD's flash flood and the Federation of Writers (Scotland) 2020 anthology. Her work in progress is set in the Outer Hebrides, where she spent time as a child.

Leonie Charlton lives in Argyll. Publications include her poetry pamphlet *Ten Minutes of Weather Away* (Cinnamon Press 2021), and travel memoir *Marram* (Sandstone Press 2020), which was Waterstones' April 2022 'Scottish Book of the Month'. Leonie is currently doing a practice-based PhD with UHI looking at Scotland's deer dilemma. **www.leoniecharlton.co.uk**

F. E. Clark lives in Scotland. She writes, paints, and takes photographs – inspired by nature in all its forms. With a story on the best fifty British and Irish Flash Fiction 2019–2020 list, she is a Best of the Net, Best Small Fictions, and 2 x Pushcart nominee. **www.feclark.weebly.com**

Alison Cohen lives in Glasgow and is a mentee on the Clydebuilt 14 Verse Apprenticeship scheme, mentored by J. L. Williams. Publications in which her poems appear include *Poetry Scotland*, *Gutter* and *14*. She won the Hugh Miller Poetry Competition in 2020 and the Federation of Writers (Scotland) Prize in 2022.

Lucy Cunningham is an emerging writer from Carluke, Lanarkshire. She received a bachelor's degree in Journalism, Creative Writing and Spanish from the University of Strathclyde, where she is currently studying for an MLitt in Creative Writing. This is her first publication.

Claire Deans is originally from Glasgow but currently lives and works in Dumfries and Galloway. She has had her poetry and short stories published in various literary magazines including *Skinklin Star*, *Cutting Teeth*, *Gutter*, *literallystories2014*. She is busy redrafting her first novel along with a collection of short stories.

B. A. Didcock was born in Edinburgh, where he now lives, but grew up in rural Cumbria, where he gathered stories and scars. He recently graduated with Distinction from Napier University's Creative Writing MA and earlier studied Medieval History at St Andrews University. He also pilots fledgling imprint Bad Gateway Press.

Samantha Dooey-Miles writes fiction that explores the significance seemingly small moments can hold. She is particularly interested in shame, embarrassment, and female rage. Her stories have been published in *Gutter*, *Postbox* and *Severine*, amongst others. In 2021 she won a Scottish Book Trust New Writer Award.

John Duffy is a Glaswegian long settled in Huddersfield. He is one of the founders of the Albert Poets, running workshops and readings for over thirty years. His latest collection, *A Gowpen*, is published by Calder Valley Poetry.

Thomas Elson's stories appear in numerous venues, including *Mad Swirl*, *Blink-Ink*, *Ellipsis*, *Scapegoat*, *Bull*, *Cabinet of Heed*, *Flash Frontier*, *Ginosko*, *Short Édition*, *Litro*, *Journal of Expressive Writing*, *Dead Mule School*, *Selkie*, *New Ulster*, *Lampeter*, and *Adelaide*. He divides his time between Northern California and Western Kansas.

Ophira Gottlieb grew up in Glasgow, moved to Yorkshire, and soon afterwards began compulsively writing poetry about hill-tops and men who drink Tetley's. Most of her poetry is set in a valley that is slowly filling with water, while the inhabitants carry on with their lives as if it isn't.

Hamish Gray is a Scottish writer studying Creative Writing at the University of Oxford. When crafting prose, he enjoys taking moments from his own life and heavily exaggerating the emotions they inspire to create a new resonance. He believes creative expression to be an essential tool for self-discovery.

Julie Laing is a Glasgow-based writer and artist. She has been published in *New Writing Scotland*, *Gutter*, *Studies in Photography* and elsewhere. Julie was a Clydebuilt 13 mentee and in 2022 won the Wigtown Poetry Prize. She coordinates off-page, a series of visual poetry exhibitions, with CD Boyland, and a peer-led criticism group supported by Street Level Photoworks.

Nicole Le Marie is from Fife and currently lives in Tottenham, London. Her writing has been published in *Lallans*, *Poetry Scotland*, *thi wurd*, *Deus Ex Machina*, longlisted for the 2022 Bridport Prize First Novel Award and highly commended in the Great Place Falkirk short story competition.

Pippa Little is a Scots poet, reviewer and editor settled in Northumberland. Her third full collection, *Time Begins to Hurt*, came out from Arc in 2022. She is a Hawthornden and Royal Literary Fund Fellow soon to become a poetry tutor for the Faber Academy in Newcastle.

Marcas Mac an Tuairneir writes in Gaelic, English and Polari. *Dùileach* and *Polaris* were shortlisted for Na Duaisean Litreachais and the Scottish Poetry Book of the Year award, respectively, in 2022. In 2023 he received a Scottish Gaelic Award for Gaelic arts and culture. *Cruinneachadh*, an anthology of poetry in translation, is out now.

Rob McClure's creative work has appeared in *Chapman*, *Gutter*, *Barcelona Review*, *Manchester Review* and other magazines. His novel, *The Scotsman*, is forthcoming from Black Springs Press in the summer of 2023. Originally from Glasgow, he currently teaches film at Knox College in the United States.

Gillean McDougall worked in classical music and broadcasting before completing the MLitt and Doctor of Fine Arts degrees in creative writing at the University of Glasgow. She writes memoir and fiction and is editor of the collaborative archive projects *Honest Error*, *Writing the Asylum* and *the prescription*.

Mora Maclean hails from Glasgow. She's had poetry published in various magazines and anthologies, including *New Writing Scotland* 23, *Poetry Scotland*, *The Dark Horse*, etc., and was a prizewinner in the Wigtown Poetry Competition in 2009. She hopes to publish a collection one day, her health and thrawn muse permitting.

Crìsdean MacIlleBhàin/Christopher Whyte will be publishing two new novels, *Beyond the Labyrinth* and *Towards Awakening*, with Cloud Machineries Press in autumn 2023. His eighth poetry collection, *Mo Shearmon / What I Have To Say*, has just come out from Francis Boutle Publishers. A sixth book of translations from the Russian of Marina Tsvetaeva, *Head on a Gleaming Plate*, appeared with Shearsman Books last year and this year a seventh will follow, *The Scale By Which You Measure Me*. **www.christopherwhyte.com, www.cloudmachineriespress.com**

Kevin MacNeil was born and raised in the Outer Hebrides. He is an award-winning writer (poet, novelist, dramatist) and is a Lecturer in Creative Writing at the University of Stirling. He has authored six books, edited a similar number, and written for television, radio, theatre, and film. Macy Starfield is one of the central characters in his novel *The Brilliant & Forever*. **www.kevinmacneil.me**

Annie Muir lives in Glasgow. Her debut pamphlet, *New Year's Eve*, was published by Broken Sleep Books. She is currently working on her first collection using funding from Creative Scotland, and has a podcast – Time for one Poem – aimed at complete beginners to poetry. **@time41poem**

Chris Neilan is an award-winning writer and filmmaker based in Edinburgh. His short fiction has been widely published and nominated for several international and national awards including the Bridport Prize, the Pushcart Prize, the Shirley Jackson Awards and the Aurora Prize. His novel, *Stellify*, is available from Broken Sleep Books.

Tom Newlands is a winner of the London Writer's Award for Literary Fiction, a Creative Future Writer's Award and New Writing North's A Writing Chance. He was a featured writer at the Scottish Mental Health Arts Festival 2022. His debut novel *Only Here, Only Now* is forthcoming in May 2024.

Cáit O'Neill McCullagh started writing poetry, at home in Ross-shire, in December 2020. Over fifty of her poems have been published online and in print. A co-winner of *Dreich*'s 'Classic Chapbook 2022', with co-author Sinéad McClure, her first full-length collection will be published by Drunk Muse Press in early 2024. **linktr.ee/caitjomac**

Alistair Paul is based in the Isle of Arran, although he is originally from Glasgow. His fascination with Arran's history and culture prompted him to learn Gaelic and eventually to use the language creatively. He is interested in traditional story-telling techniques and weaves these into contemporary themes in his writing.

Andy Raffan was shortlisted for the Edinburgh Award for Flash Fiction in 2022 and 2023. He has had poetry published by Soor Ploom Press, and flash fiction by *Ink Sweat & Tears*. He is a member of the Strathkelvin Writers Group, and is studying for an Open University Creative Writing degree.

Martin Raymond lives in Milnathort. He has an MLitt and PhD in Creative Writing, both from the University of Stirling. His work has been published in *New Writing Scotland* and has been shortlisted for the V. S. Pritchett Short Story Prize and longlisted for the Watson, Little x Indie Novella Prize.

Julie Rea is an award-winning short fiction writer from Glasgow. She has been placed and shortlisted in many competitions, including the Bath Short Story Award and the Cambridge Short Story Prize, and is widely published in literary journals and anthologies. Her fiction has been nominated for the Pushcart Prize.

Nicola Rose lives and writes in rural Lanarkshire. She has a Masters degree in Creative Writing with Distinction from the University of Strathclyde, and in 2020 won the Beatrice Colin Memorial Award for the best undergraduate dissertation in Creative Writing. Her work has recently appeared in issue 27 of *Gutter*.

Neil Gordon Shaw lives in Edinburgh. His memoir, *Beyond Grey*, about three years in post-communist Poland, won the Scottish Association of Writers Non-Fiction Book of the Year and the Moniack Mhor Travel Writing Award. Neil has recently completed a collection of short stories. He is on Twitter **@neil_writing**.

Amy Stewart is a writer living in the Scottish Borders. She was the winner of the New Writing North & Word Factory Northern Apprentice Award in 2021 and the Mairtín Crawford Prize for Short Story in 2022. She is represented by Marilia Savvides at 42mp.

Lynn Valentine lives in the Black Isle with greedy labradors. Her debut poetry collection, *Life's Stink and Honey*, was published by Cinnamon Press in 2022 after winning their literature award. Her Scots language pamphlet, *A Glimmer o Stars*, was published by Hedgehog Press in 2021 after winning their dialect award.

Ryan Van Winkle is an author, artist and producer based in Edinburgh. His second collection, *The Good Dark*, won the Saltire Society's 2015 Poetry Book of the Year award. His work has appeared in *The American Poetry Review*, *Modern Poetry in Translation*, and *Gutter*.

Katie Webster lives in Caithness where she works as an occupational therapist. She has previously published short fiction in *New Writing Scotland*.

Edinburgh-based **Jay Whittaker** has published two poetry collections with Cinnamon Press, *Sweet Anaesthetist* (2020), and her Saltire Award-winning debut *Wristwatch* (2017). She is widely published (credits include *Poetry Review*, *The Scotsman*, *The North*, *Butcher's Dog*, *The Rialto*, and the Bloodaxe anthology *Staying Human*).